Savannah's Bluebird

Lori Crane

Lori Crane Entertainment
www.LoriCrane.com

This book is a work of fiction. All names, characters, places, and incidents are products of the author's imagination.

ISBN 978-0-9883545-8-6
eBook ISBN 978-0-9883545-9-3

SAVANNAH'S BLUEBIRD

Table of Contents

Dedicated to my beautiful son

Trien Duong

June 15, 1981 - February 24, 2014

You will always be the brightest star in our sky

Chapter 1

The bells rang from atop the steeple as Savannah struggled to pull open the ancient wooden door of the church. When she entered, she saw the backs of the heads of dozens of people sitting in the pews. She stopped in the vestibule and awaited the organ music to announce her entrance. She ran her gloved hand over her dark brown hair, adjusted her pillbox hat, pulled the tulle veil over her face, and smoothed down her ivory wedding gown. In her other hand, she clutched a dainty bouquet of white roses with sprays of baby's breath. The smell filled her nostrils.

After a few moments, the organist at the front of the church played a fanfare and immediately followed with the "Wedding March." She inhaled deeply and took a small step forward. After a pause, she took another step…and another. She hesitated, thinking it strange that the crowd didn't rise and turn to face her. She inched forward again, pausing between steps. Surely the congregation would rise when the minister instructed them to do so, but she didn't know what he was waiting for. She put a smile on her face as she admired the sun shining through the stained-glass windows, creating a mosaic of bright colors across the room, but as she reached the halfway mark of her grand entrance, the room darkened. The sun had disappeared behind a cloud, and the vibrant colors that bathed the room turned a dismal shade of gray. Her smile vanished also.

It was difficult to see through the netted veil, but she could have sworn she saw something large sitting in the center of the altar. She narrowed her eyes and, yes indeed, something was there. At the top of three small steps that led up to the altar, a white coffin rested in front of the minister's podium. It was surrounded by beautiful sprays of flowers—roses, carnations, chrysanthemums, daisies. The sight reminded her of her father's funeral and her head swam with the painful memory. She looked down at her bouquet and closed her eyes for a moment. When she opened them again, her breath caught deep in her chest as she watched her beautiful white roses faded from white to gray to black—black and dead. The leaves shriveled and a few of the petals gently fell from their stems, fluttering to the floor. She tightly clutched the bouquet and quickly pulled her left hand away when a thorn poked through her glove and punctured the skin of her palm. She saw the small hole in the satin fabric, but there was no blood.

She squeezed her hand into a fist to make the pain stop, and looked back up at the altar. Why was there a coffin on the altar, and where was August? Why was her groom not there to greet her? She staggered a bit as she took another step forward. The

"Wedding March" kept pounding from the organ and she kept inching forward. She placed her hand over her heart in an effort to make it beat normally. Remembering the puncture wound, she looked down at her dress to make sure there was no blood on the bodice. She stopped dead in her tracks.

Her beautiful wedding gown was no longer ivory; it was now black. She thought she would faint, and looked up to search the crowd for someone to help her. When she looked through the mesh of her veil, she noticed it too had turned black. Panic rose in her chest and her throat constricted. The next breath wouldn't come. She felt her knees quiver and she didn't know if she could take another step. Her mouth opened and closed like that of a fish gasping for air, but she couldn't form any words. She looked left and right at her family and friends, but no one looked back at her. They all stared straight ahead. It was as if they didn't see her.

She stumbled forward a few more steps and noticed her soon-to-be stepdaughter, Emma, sitting alone in the second pew. She approached Emma and noticed tears running down the girl's face, dripping off her chin and leaving dark spots on her pink cotton dress. She reached toward Emma, but stopped when the "Wedding March" turned into Chopin's "Funeral March." She looked up at the organ on the right side of the altar, but the organist did not look back at her.

Was Savannah in the wrong place?

She spun around in what felt like slow motion and looked at the stained-glass windows, the pews, the high, scallop-shaped ceiling. No, this was her childhood church—Fisherman's Church. She had been coming here since she was a baby. Was she here on the wrong date? She turned again and looked at the people. She knew every one of them. She had invited every one of them. She knew it was August 25, 1936—her wedding day. Why was Emma here at a funeral? Why was she crying? More importantly, who was in the coffin?

She spun again and faced the coffin on the altar. Was she losing her mind? Where was August? Terror filled her as adrenaline rose like flames up the back of her neck.

Two men she had never seen before, dressed in black suits, stepped forward and gently opened the coffin's lid, and Savannah saw the inside of the lid was lined with blood-red satin. *Who is in there?* And why was there a funeral here on her wedding day?

She climbed the three steps to the altar and placed her hand on the side of the coffin. She reluctantly looked inside.

It was a woman—a dark-haired woman in an ivory wedding dress.

She gazed down into her own face and heard a scream escape her lips.

Chapter 2

She woke to the distant, incessant sound of a barking dog. For a moment, she thought she was still in the middle of the nightmare and wanted to cry out for help, but the continual barking meant her dog was once again on the wrong side of the door. Her eyes snapped open. Was she awake? Was the awful dream over? She bolted upright in bed and put her left hand on her chest, but then pulled it away and looked at her palm for a puncture wound. There was none. She wiped the sweat from her upper lip and looked around the room, assuring herself it had only been a nightmare and it was over. She closed her eyes tightly and shook her head to shake off the memory of seeing her own face in the coffin. She exhaled and fell back onto her pillow.

After a few minutes, she felt her breathing return to normal. She peeked at the drawn curtains and saw slivers of sunlight sneaking in around the edges of the heavy fabric. She heard the faucet in the bathroom sink turn on for a moment, then off again. She could smell the fresh scent of soap. August always woke before her.

Though it was highly inappropriate, she had moved in, unmarried, with August last summer. Girls didn't do things like that, but she wasn't a girl. She was grown woman of thirty-one years who refused to live her life according to old-fashioned tradition. She did, however, have her own room, which shared a connecting bathroom with August's room.

She kicked off the blanket, sat up, and placed her feet on the floor. She frowned as she looked around at the state of the room. The deep mahogany furniture and royal blue velvet settee was contrasted by the dirty clothes strewn about the floor. She curled her toes into the burgundy rug and pouted. She knew she would need to be a better housekeeper than this if she wanted to keep a man happy. That's what her mother always said, anyway.

Savannah doubted she would find the time to clean the room today. After all, it was her wedding day. She prayed it would turn out better than the terrible dream she'd just endured. She wiped sleep out of the corners of her eyes, pinched her cheeks to make them appear rosy, and combed her fingers through her tangled hair in a futile attempt to tame it. She used to wrap it in a braid before bed, as her mother taught her, but the short hairstyles of the last decade wouldn't allow that. Since she'd given in to social pressure and gotten hers cut, she always woke to a mess of hair, and wondered why women would ever let others in New York and Paris dictate styles, especially styles that didn't work for normal people. She rose, wrapped her silk robe around her, and padded across the rug toward the bathroom door. She stopped at the open doorway, leaned her shoulder against the doorframe, and crossed her arms over her chest. A smile crossed her lips as she watched August. The sight of him instantly took away any discomfort the dream had left.

What a remarkable man she was marrying. Her heart felt like it would burst at the sight of him. He was ruggedly handsome and did not fit the stereotype of a pasty lawyer. He looked more like that movie star Cary Grant. August's jet-black hair and warm, dark-chocolate eyes sat atop a mischievous dimpled smile usually seen on womanizers. He was not, however, anything of the sort. He was a kind and generous man, filled with every quality a good man could possibly possess. He did things like open doors for women, make coffee in the morning, and pick up fresh muffins from the bakery on his way to work. Everyone loved August, especially his staff at the law office. He had an admiration for simple things like sunsets and campfires, but also a drive for finer things like his brand new Plymouth Coupe and renting French villas for family holidays. He told Savannah he hoped to own a villa someday. He'd always wanted to speak French, and last summer he'd taken a few lessons from an elderly woman in town who had moved from Paris a few years ago.

He stood in front of the foggy mirror, white shaving cream lathered on his face, his head cocked as he shaved. He wore only a white towel around his waist, and his slim physique, created from years of tennis in high school and college, made her heart beat faster. He didn't stop shaving when he saw her, but he gave her his familiar wink.

"Good morning, Mrs. Ryan. I didn't wake you, did I?" He looked at her in the mirror and his gaze pierced her very soul.

She shook her head, thinking "Mrs. Ryan" had a very nice ring to it. The way he looked at her, like a jungle cat watching its prey, gave her tingles in the pit of her stomach. It also made her self-conscious. She never considered herself a great beauty, not even casually pretty, and couldn't for the life of her figure out what he saw in her.

"Good," he continued. "You need to be well rested for today. Are you ready?"

"As ready as I'll ever be, I guess. It only took us ten years," she replied, moving in front of him toward the far sink and reaching for her toothbrush in the ceramic holder.

Times like this made her appreciate the fact that August made enough money for them to have amenities like two sinks in their bathroom, especially when the rest of the country still suffered from the devastation triggered by the stock market crash a few years ago. Even with the luxury, he had to step back a little to allow her room to reach the toothpaste.

"Only ten years?" August teased. "If you remember correctly, I asked you to marry me twenty years ago under your dad's apple tree."

She sighed, closed her eyes in front of the foggy mirror, and absentmindedly began brushing her teeth. She could picture that big old apple tree like it was right in front of her. The branches spread out across the sky like an enormous umbrella shading the picnic table beneath it. At the end of a good summer, so many apples would be on the tree, the branches would almost touch the ground, burdened by the weight. The old paint-peeled table beneath the tree was a favorite place for the squirrels to sit and eat the apples, leaving half-eaten cores when they scampered off. August and Savannah spent many, many afternoons talking and playing and telling childhood secrets under that tree.

In the warmth of one late fall afternoon, Savannah sat alone at the picnic table with an array of colored silk threads spread out in front of her. The leaves had fallen a few weeks ago, leaving only a few stray apples on the ends of the branches. The sun shone through the branches, warming her face and hands, and the sweet smell of decaying apples and the crisp smell of dying leaves surrounded her, making her head swim with happiness. Fall was her favorite time of year. She stared at the woven fabric she was embroidering and sorted through the colored threads on the table.

An ocean inlet ran along the back of the property, and she could faintly hear the soft babble of the water splashing on the rocks, as well as the buzz of dragonflies and katydids. August appeared out of the dying brush that was only a few weeks ago thick summer bushes. He was wearing a brown button-up shirt, suspenders, and dirty trousers darkened by wetness up to the knees. Obviously, he had been playing at the inlet, probably trying to catch frogs or crawdads. He ran over to the picnic table and plopped down across from her.

"Watcha doin'?" He was short-winded from running.

"I'm working on a pillow covering for home economics class," she answered.

She picked up the fabric, turned it around,

and held it up for his approval.

He wrinkled his forehead and said, "It looks like a bird. I thought you liked dogs."

"I do like dogs, but Mrs. Thompson said we have to create something that flies." She rolled her eyes and placed it back in front of her on the table.

"Well, why don't you sew a spaceship with a robot or something?" he asked, wrinkling his forehead.

"Only boys would make spaceships and robots." She scowled at him. "I want to make something else. My dad told me this story about a bluebird. He said a gypsy woman told him the bluebird represents love, and if you're with someone you love and see a bluebird, you'll be with that person forever." She picked up the blue thread and attempted to thread her needle. "So, I'm embroidering a bluebird."

"Was it one of those gypsies down on the beach?"

"No, he said it was a gypsy woman in New Orleans a long time ago—before I was even born. He was working on the railroad down there when he met my mother. He said the day after the gypsy told him that story, he and momma saw a bluebird. They were married a few days later."

When August didn't respond, she looked up at him—and froze. Right above his head, on the lowest branch of the tree, sat a little bluebird. It was bright blue on top with a reddish-brown throat, and it was no more than a foot from them. She didn't move, half afraid of scaring it away and half amazed that their conversation topic had suddenly manifested itself. August turned to follow her gaze and froze also. Neither of them dared breathe as they watched the bird—and the bird watched them.

"Will you hand me that towel?" August asked.

Savannah didn't respond.

"Savannah, hello? Will you please hand me that towel?" August asked again, snapping Savannah's attention back to the present.

"I'm sorry," Savannah said, handing August the white fluffy towel from the side of the vanity. "I was just thinking about that old apple tree." She rinsed her toothbrush and placed it back in the holder. "A lot of water has passed under the bridge since those days. Are you sure you want to marry me today?" Savannah giggled nervously. She tried to sound as if she was kidding, but deep inside, she was feeling insecure. After all, he did marry someone else before her. It wasn't his fault Savannah didn't live in Biloxi back then, but did he really have to completely forget about her and marry a beautiful blonde who looked more like a fashion model than a wife?

Eula was a stunning woman. She had a sense of style that rivaled that of the most elite Paris models. She came from a well-to-do family and was highly educated, had traveled the world, and most importantly, gave August a precious daughter. Eula was not only beautiful when they married, but now she always would be. She passed away before her time, and the only things left of her were wonderful memories and stunning photographs in which she would never age or get saggy. How could anyone compete with that? Especially someone like Savannah—mousy, unorganized, clumsy.

She giggled in an attempt to hide her insecurity, but she knew August sensed it. After all, this was not the first time he had seen it in her face or heard it in her voice. She hated that he knew her weakness.

She watched him slowly wipe his face with the towel. He set it on the counter and turn to her. He moved in front of her, sat down on the edge of the vanity, and gently took both her hands in his. He looked down at them for a moment, his thumbs brushing across her knuckles, and then he pulled them to his lips and kissed them one at a time. He lifted his eyes to meet hers without lifting his head. The look gave her goose bumps.

"Savannah, I want to marry you today. I've loved you since we were children. I will love you when we're old and gray. I will love you forever, for all of eternity."

They stood motionless for a long time, staring into each other's eyes.

In a few short hours, she would have everything she had always hoped for. They would finally be man and wife.

Chapter 3

While Savannah bathed and dressed, August went downstairs and started breakfast. By the time she came down the stairs, the house smelled delightful with the aroma of rich coffee and fresh toast. The smell made her mouth water. The morning sun streamed through the windows on either side of the front door and painted bright lines across the polished oak floor. Savannah paused and glanced out one of the windows. She saw no clouds in the sky and was thrilled it would be a beautiful day.

She entered the kitchen and saw a pitcher of freshly squeeze orange juice on the tiled island. August handed her a hot cup of coffee. She sipped it as she watched him remove slices of warm, crisp bread from the toaster, cut them diagonally, and place them on a china dish on the island. He then pulled two silver knives from the drawer and placed them next to the butter and jam. She laughed at that, knowing he could never bring himself to use the same knife on both condiments. Getting butter in the jam or jam in the butter made him squeamish, despite the fact he could mix both on a piece of toast without a thought. Yes, he was a perfectionist. She was not.

Savannah grabbed a half slice of toast and covered it in butter and jam, using the different knives. She sat down at the breakfast table at the far end of the kitchen, in front of a wall of doors and windows. The windows were floor to ceiling in the two-story room, and in the middle of the wall stood two french doors that led to the patio. She glanced into the backyard at the crisp fall morning, took another sip of coffee, and turned back to him. "So, what are your plans for this morning?"

August placed his empty coffee cup in the sink and straightened his wide tie as he approached the table. "I have to run by the office and get some paperwork finished for the senior partners. I don't want anything to disturb our honeymoon, and with this hearing coming up on Monday, I need to get this done today. Those gypsies are fighting the proposed location of the new golf course, and Judge Martin is going to hear the case and make a ruling. I shouldn't be at the office more than an hour or so. We just need to cross the Ts and dot the Is." He grinned at her as he reached for his suit coat hanging on the back of the dining chair. "*Then* I'm going to change into my tuxedo, go to Fisherman's Church, and marry my childhood sweetheart."

She grinned. He was so handsome as a young boy. Today, more than twenty years later, he was even more so, and today she would finally be Mrs. August Ryan. She was so happy, she was uncharacteristically speechless as she watched him.

"What about you?" he asked as he put on his coat.

She felt a momentary surge of panic and pulled her appointment book from her purse on the table. She opened it, turned a few pages, and read, "I'm picking up Emma from Sally's house at nine thirty, getting a manicure at ten, we're getting our hair done at eleven, and we're picking up the flowers at twelve. If all goes smoothly, we may even have time for a quick lunch in town before Mary and Billy get here to take us to the church. If not, we'll just grab a bite here before we leave."

"Is there anything you need me to do?" he asked as he placed his black fedora on his head.

She shook her head, closing her appointment book. "No, I think I have it all under control."

She rose from the chair, moved toward him, and wrapped her arms around his shoulders. He entwined his arms around her waist and lowered his head to kiss her. Just before their lips met, he stopped. When she opened her eyes, he smiled and gave her a wink. Her knees grew weak. It was a good thing he had his arms around her or else she would've ended up sprawled on the floor like a rag doll.

He gave her a quick but tender kiss. "I'll see you at the church, Mrs. Ryan. Two o'clock. Don't be late."

"I wouldn't miss it for the world, Mr. Ryan," she replied and stretched up on her toes to kiss him again.

He pulled away from her, and she watched him as he sauntered toward the front door. With his right hand, he grabbed the garment bag containing his tuxedo off the coat rack, and with his left hand, his briefcase off the floor. He threw the garment bag over his shoulder without breaking stride. He moved like a thoroughbred stallion heading out to the field, a dancer in a well-choreographed routine, a tiger strolling through the brush. He opened the door, turned back to her for a moment, and mouthed, "Two o'clock."

She nodded and he was gone.

Chapter 4

No sooner had the front door closed than the telephone blared from the kitchen wall. Savannah jumped.

She put her hand on her chest and murmured, "Wow, I must be a little jittery today. Good thing I didn't have my coffee cup in my hand." She removed her hand from her chest and looked down at it, remembering the horrible dream. She shook her head as the telephone rang a second time. She rounded the island, reaching for the phone, and accidentally knocked over the pitcher of orange juice. It splashed all over the island, drenching the freshly made toast and covering the butter and jam, before dripping onto the floor.

"Oh, no!" she moaned.

The telephone rang a third time.

"Hello?" she said as she simultaneously grabbed the phone from the wall and reached for a towel from the cabinet under the sink.

"Hello, Miss Blakely? This is Beatrice calling from the salon," the caller said.

"Hello, Beatrice. I'm not late, am I?" Savannah glanced at the clock above the sink while she sopped up the juice from the island.

"Oh, no, no, you're not late. I do have some bad news for you, though. Your manicurist called in sick today, and the only other manicurist I have available today doesn't have an opening until two o'clock."

"Two o'clock? Um, no, that isn't going to work. I'm getting married at two o'clock." Savannah stopped wiping, put down the towel, and held up her hand to look at her nails.

They weren't too bad, but they certainly were not perfect like Eula's would be. Everything about Eula had always been perfect, even her nails. Damn.

"Isn't there anything else you can do this morning? It's my wedding day," Savannah asked.

"No, I'm very sorry. We're booked solid until two," the receptionist replied.

Obviously Beatrice wasn't going to be any help, so Savannah gave up.

"All right, then. Thank you for calling."

Savannah was saying good-bye when Boomer jumped on the glass door and began barking. Again Savannah jumped. "What is wrong with me today?"

"I'm sorry? I didn't understand what..." Beatrice said.

"Oh, nothing, I'm sorry. My dog is barking. I have to run."

Beatrice began saying something about calling in the next few days to reschedule, but Savannah again interrupted her. "I'm going to be on my honeymoon for the next week. I have to go now. I'll call when I get back in town. Thank you for calling, Beatrice. Good-bye."

Boomer was like a dog possessed, barking and jumping incessantly on the door, covering it with muddy streaks. Savannah hung up the phone and dropped the towel on the kitchen table as she passed it on her way to open the door. Boomer bounced in and jumped on her with full force, muddy paws and all.

Boomer was a sweet, lovable ball of gray and white fluff. He was part sheepdog and part mutt. He didn't have a ferocious bone in his body, but he could quite possibly smother one to death with affection. He also had a bad habit of digging up the flowers that Savannah tried so very hard to grow. This made it necessary to bath him regularly, and his long fur needed to be brushed daily. It was a good thing Savannah loved to brush him.

"No, Boomer, get down," she scolded, but it was too late. Her mint green cotton dress was covered in brown paw prints. "What is wrong with you, crazy dog? And where did all this mud come from? You were digging in my garden again, weren't you? Bad dog." Savannah frowned at the dog, who was wagging his tail and panting, oblivious to being chastised. She grabbed him by the collar and led him toward the pantry.

"Do you want some breakfast, boy?" she asked in a voice usually reserved for a two-year-old. "You need to come in the pantry and eat, because we can't have this mud all over the house. I guess since my manicure was canceled, I have time to get you cleaned up and"—Savannah looked down at her dress—"get myself cleaned up, too."

Savannah entered the pantry with her fingers locked tightly around Boomer's collar. She reached for his food bag with her free hand but found it empty. She shook the bag as if it would magically fill itself with dog food.

"Oh, no, why don't you have any food, Boomer?"

He barked.

"What in the world are you going to eat?" She looked down at him.

His tail wagged.

"This is just no good. I certainly don't have time to give you a bath, change my clothes, clean up this mess, *and* go to the store for dog food."

She glanced out the pantry door into the kitchen, where the orange juice was still dripping off the island and soaking the floor, wondering what she could whip together to feed the hungry dog. Boomer wiggled out of her grasp, ran over to the island, and started licking up the juice from the floor.

"Boomer, no!" she yelled, wondering if orange juice was bad for dogs.

He continued licking.

She grabbed some dog treats from the shelf and tossed them toward Boomer. "Maybe that will hold you over until I get back from the store."

She stepped out of the pantry, looked at the clock above the sink, and knew there wouldn't be enough time to get all the chores done before she had to pick up Emma. She suddenly felt overwhelmed and frustrated. She moved a step out of the pantry and leaned her back against the wall. She slowly slid down until she was sitting on the floor, and she watched the muddy dog licking the juice. She wanted to cry.

Just as she was about to give in to the tears, the front door opened and a female voice sang out, "Helloooo?"

"I'm in the kitchen," Savannah yelled back. "Or what's left of it."

Mary Taylor, Savannah's little sister, popped around the corner. "What do you mean, what's left…" Mary stopped when she saw the mess.

Boomer casually glanced at Mary, wagged his tail, and then ignored her as he continued licking juice and gobbling dog treats.

"Oh, Savvy-girl, what in the world happened here?" Mary asked with a grimace on her face, but trying to stifle a giggle.

"I don't know," Savannah said. "August left for work, and the moment he walked out the door, everything fell apart."

Mary took Boomer by the collar and led him to the door. "Come on, Boomer, you need to go outside. It looks like Auntie Mary has some work to do." She led him outside and closed the door behind him. The dog sat down on the other side of the door, sadly looking inside.

Mary turned her attention to Savannah. "Looks like you need a little help. I'll tell you what, I'll get busy and clean this mess up." She offered her hand to help Savannah up off the floor and frowned at her dirty dress. "You need to go upstairs and change."

"The salon just called and canceled my manicure." Savannah pouted as she rose. She held out her hands and examined her nails again. "I guess the manicurist called in sick, and they don't have anyone else to do my nails this morning."

"Oh, no," Mary said.

"And," Savannah continued, "Boomer is all muddy and apparently out of dog food." Savannah waved the empty bag in the air. "I guess with all the wedding planning, I forgot to add dog food to the shopping list." Savannah sighed. "I hate it when I overlook something so simple, especially today when there's so much to do."

"Oh, nonsense. Relax and I'll help you. It's your wedding day. You can't be stressed on your wedding day. I'll stop by the store, pick up some dog food, and take Boomer home with me so Billy can give him a bath. What else do you have to do this morning, and why did August go into work on his wedding day?"

"He had to finish some paperwork about that new golf course. They need some documents for a court hearing on Monday."

"What kind of hearing do they need to build a golf course?"

"I don't know. Something about the people who live there."

"Those gypsies? They've been there for twenty years."

"I know, but I guess the mayor wants them off the land, and apparently they need the judge to make that happen." Savannah shrugged. "August said it would only take him an hour or so to finish it up. I need to go pick up Emma…" Savannah stopped and looked at the clock. "Oh, no! What time is it?

Mary removed her gloves and looked down at her watch. "Nine fifteen. Why?"

"I'm supposed to pick up Emma at nine thirty. How am I going to get all this done when time is just slipping away?"

Mary dropped her gloves on the table and grabbed the towel to finish cleaning up the juice. "Don't fret. Little sister to the rescue. You just have wedding jitters. Take a deep breath, go change your dress, and do what you have to do. I'll take care of everything else. We have lots of time to get back here and get you and Emma to the church."

With a sigh of relief, Savannah said, "Thank you, Mary. I don't know what I'd do without you."

Mary gave her a reassuring smile as she grabbed another towel from under the sink. "How often does my only sister get married? Now go get changed."

Savannah ran upstairs and returned in a few minutes in a freshly pressed powder-blue dress and matching cloche hat. Mary had just finished wiping up juice when Savannah entered the kitchen.

"Okay, I'm dressed now for the second time, and I'm going to pick up Emma. Are you sure you have this under control?" Savannah asked.

"Yes, it'll all be fine. Now go." Mary shooed her away with her right hand.

"Okay, then. Emma and I are going to get our hair done and pick up the flowers. We'll grab some lunch at the café in town and be back here by one o'clock." Savannah picked up her purse from the dining table. "Are you sure this isn't too much?" Savannah looked around at the mess and eyed Boomer, who was still sitting right outside the glass door.

"It's no problem at all," Mary said as she

moved around the counter and reached for her sister. "Savannah, before you go...I haven't had much time to talk to you the last few weeks, but I need to tell you how much I think Momma and Daddy would love to be here today. They both loved August, and I know after Daddy died, it broke Momma's heart to take us all the way to New Orleans, away from our friends, and especially away from August." Mary started to tear up. "Anyway, Momma and Daddy would be very, very happy today."

Savannah looked at Mary and didn't respond. So many mixed feelings were trying to come to the surface, but now was not the time to figure them out. Today was certainly not the day to second-guess their mother and the decision she made about how to raise two girls alone. Their father had died so suddenly, a few weeks after he told Savannah the bluebird story.

Thomas Blakely had worked for the Southern Pacific Railroad since he was a teenager. They built countless stations and laid miles and miles of track across the South. He had been working in New Orleans as a young man, relaying some track the vagabonds had destroyed. That's where he met Savannah's mother.

Gertrude was a girl of sixteen waiting tables at her parents' restaurant in the French Quarter. Thomas said when Gertrude waited on his table one afternoon, he gazed upon her lovely face and immediately knew there would be no other woman for him. He said she had sparkling eyes and a lovely smile. He spent every day working long hours in the hot Louisiana sun and every night following her around town. He camped out on her Lakeview doorstep, followed her to school, and even started showing up at church on Sundays. Later, she said he made quite a pest of himself, but she was flattered by the attention, especially since he was a handsome boy from Biloxi. She had never travelled more than a few blocks away from her childhood home, and this boy was made even more attractive by possessing the ability to whisk her away to another life. Gertrude admitted later it was love at first sight for her, too.

When Savannah was thirteen and Mary was eleven, their father went to work one day and didn't return home. A messenger knocked on their door and told their mother an accident had occurred and Thomas had been killed. The girls watched their mother collapse in the floor. Savannah had never been so scared at the sight of her mother crying, but she put on a brave front to comfort her little sister. From that moment, she felt like she became the adult in the household. Her mother had trouble getting out of bed some days, and Savannah saw her swallowing pills on occasion. Her little sister Mary had always been a shy girl, but after their father died, the little thing never said a word to anyone. Savannah hated to see Mary's big, round eyes brimming with tears, but that was the only response she saw from Mary for the next few months.

Since their father had worked for the railroad company for so long, one would have thought they'd take care of his family financially after his death, but Savannah was sure that didn't happened. The girls were never told any details of the accident or the aftermath. All they knew was one day their father was there and the next he was gone, and their mother was in great distress and was taking something called lithium like it was candy. When Gertrude managed to crawl out of bed, Savannah noticed her speech was often slurred and her hands trembled all the time.

Two months later, Savannah found herself, her sister, and her mother struggling to tote all their belongings onto a train bound for New Orleans—the same train her father used to work for. They arrived at the same depot where her parents met fifteen years earlier and once there, they were met by Savannah's grandparents.

Chapter 5

After Daddy died, Momma's idea of moving to New Orleans to be near Grandma and Grandpa was the worst decision ever made in the eyes of a thirteen-year-old girl. At that age, Savannah was just beginning to stretch her wings. She felt she was a gangly, homely teenager, but she was looking forward to school dances and starting high school, maybe even trying out for the women's softball team, though she knew she was more a klutz than an athlete. She didn't understand her mother's decision to uproot her and Mary from their home. And Louisiana? How far away was Louisiana? She had only been to the suburb of Lakeview a few times to visit her grandparents on holidays, and from what she remembered, it was very far away. Would she be able to come back and see her friends? She knew she couldn't come back daily for school, but maybe she could come back on the weekends to see August.

As it turned out, Louisiana was so far away from Biloxi and the only life Savannah had ever known, it might as well have been the moon. The streets were different, the people were different, and the school was different. Everything was strange and awful. After losing her daddy so suddenly, losing her home and her friends was too much to take. Losing her best friend August was the last straw.

Following the move, Savannah sank into a deep depression for a long time, and it took years, which translates into forever in teenage time, to get comfortable in her new surroundings. Savannah attended high school at a new school with new teachers and zero friends. This school was so much bigger than Biloxi High School, she got lost in the building every day for the first week, as well as getting lost walking home for the first month.

One evening, she wandered around the streets of Lakeview for hours before finding her way back to the house. It was dusk when she finally arrived on her doorstep, and her mother was beside herself with worry.

"Savannah, where have you been?" Her mother scolded, turning toward the sink to take another pill.

"I was on my way home. I got turned around."

"Well, you didn't get *turned around* yesterday. Why must you do things like this to me? I was worried sick."

"Momma, I'm not *doing* anything to you. I'm trying my best to not lose my mind here. I just got turned around, that's all." Savannah marched out of the kitchen and plopped down at the small reading table by the front window.

Her mother entered after a few minutes with a much softer expression on her face. "I'm sorry, Savannah. I was just worried when you were late. I didn't mean to raise my voice to you."

"It's okay, Momma. I'm sorry I got lost and was late." Savannah's bottom lip began to quiver as her eyes brimmed with tears.

Her mother reached out to her with a shaking hand, but Savannah turned away and ran up the stairs to her room. She felt guilty for being late and worrying her mother, but she felt angry for her mother dragging her here in the first place. She hated New Orleans, and she refused to make friends. She would be going back to Biloxi soon. She didn't know how, but she knew she couldn't stay in New Orleans forever. Most of her neighbors and schoolmates were nice to her, but she didn't want anything to do with them. What was she supposed to do? Explain to her new friends how her father was dead and her mother was killing herself with pills? She refused to talk to them. The few people she did speak with were only out of necessity and the conversations were always short and to the point. She already had friends back home. She didn't need new friends. She certainly didn't want a new best friend. She felt that if she gave in and started talking to these new people, she would somehow be replacing August. She could never replace her father, and she refused to replace her best friend.

***

One Saturday morning, she strolled down to

the beach of Lake Ponchartrain and found a quiet spot on the bank. She stared at the ripples of water lapping the shore, mesmerized by the sound, which was accompanied by seabirds whistling and cawing as they flew overhead. She closed her eyes and let the sounds wash over her, attempting to block out the awful world she now lived in. The noise of someone clearing her throat interrupted Savannah's reverie. She looked around and saw an old woman emerging from the tree line behind her. The woman was covered in layers of bright and ornate scarves and wraps that curled around her in the breeze. Her dark red hair was in a bun on top of her head, but stringy ringlets dripped around her face and neck, tangling themselves in her large hoop earrings.

"I thought I'd find you here." The old woman cackled as she approached.

"I'm sorry, ma'am. You must have me confused with someone else. Do I know you?"

"No, I don't have you confused with anyone else, dear, and no, you don't know me." The old woman had a bulge of tobacco in her cheek, and she spit some sweet-smelling brown juice on the dirt.

Savannah started to rise to leave, made uncomfortable by the weird old woman.

"No, chavi, you need to stay and speak with me. I came down here from Biloxi because I have a gift for you here in my bujo."

"Your bujo?"

The woman held up her large bag.

Savannah reluctantly sat back down, now curious about the woman.

"You're from Biloxi?"

"No, dear, I'm from New Orleans, but I've

lived in Biloxi a few years." The woman plopped down next to her and began digging deep into the bag. She fished around for a long time and eventually pulled out a small object wrapped in a dirty handkerchief. She looked at it strangely for a moment, and then held it toward Savannah, who did not reach for it.

"Here." She thrust it into Savannah's chest. "This is for you. Take it."

"I'm sure I don't need any gifts, ma'am."

"Just open it. It's baxtalo. You would say…lucky." She placed it in Savannah's hand.

Savannah stared at the handkerchief and didn't move.

"Open it," the crone demanded.

Savannah placed it on her lap and tried to touch the filthy handkerchief as little as possible as she unfolded it to reveal a small blue object made of glass. She held it up between her thumb and forefinger and saw it was a two-inch-tall bluebird. She turned and awaited an explanation from the old woman.

"I knew you'd like it." The woman smiled through missing teeth. She twisted her chin to the side and spit more tobacco juice onto the ground.

"But why?"

"I know you've had a difficult time since coming here, and I thought this would make you feel better." The woman turned and stared at the water. Her expression grew solemn and she continued speaking without looking at Savannah. "Fate may not be kind to you, young lady, and you will need this item to face your future."

"Ma'am, I'm sure I don't know what you're

talking about."

"Oh, you don't, do you? Tell me about Thomas Blakely."

"What?"

"Your father."

"What do you know about my father?"

"I met him about fifteen years ago…right here on this very beach." She thumbed a direction over her shoulder. "Right over there at a little watering hole I worked at. He was courting your mother at the time." She smiled. "I was young then, too, and I must admit, he was a handsome man, and I had eyes for him as well. He was working on those railroad tracks my people destroyed. They were angry that the train was going to go through their homes. I don't mean near their homes, I mean right through the middle of them. My people have always lived off the land, not in those fancy houses like you live in. It was because of us that your father was here working at the time. It was because of us he met your mother, so I guess it was because of us that you were born." She paused and kept staring at the small wavelets. "He sure was a handsome man. Too bad he wasn't one of us."

"You're a gypsy."

The woman nodded.

"Do you live on the beach in Biloxi?"

"Sometimes. Sometimes I live here."

Savannah looked down at the glass object in her hand. "You're the one who told my father the bluebird story."

"Yes, child, I am." She turned toward Savannah. "The bluebird is magical, and it can do some surprising things."

"Yes, my father told me."

The woman didn't acknowledge her comment. "Sadly, I didn't plan on him seeing the bluebird while he was with your mother. I was hoping he would see it while he was with…oh, never mind about that. Things happen and life goes on. We all have our own private destiny to live out, even if it affects others."

Savannah stared at the woman's face, realizing the woman wasn't as old as she initially looked. She carried herself like an old woman, but there wasn't a crease on her face, not a wrinkle around her eyes or lips. She was actually quite pretty in an exotic way.

"So, you were friends with my father?"

"You could say that."

Savannah didn't like the cryptic answer. Did this woman love her father? Was the bluebird story a spell to make her father fall in love?

"Tell me about August."

A shiver went up Savannah's spine. "How do you know about August?"

"I know everything, child. I know the past, the present"—she looked Savannah in the eyes—"and the future."

"Are you a fortune teller?"

The woman shrugged. "No, I am no drabarni—fortune teller, as you say." She spit again and shrugged. "Some people call me a witch, but I'm no witch, either. I just know things. Some people around here call it voodoo, but it's not voodoo. My people come from a faraway land and some of us have special gifts."

The woman slowly climbed to her feet with a few grunts and groans. She leaned forward a bit, half hunched as if her back was aching. Her scarves blew wildly around her head as the wind picked up, giving her a mysterious aura. She *looked* like a witch.

"I will tell you one thing before I go. My son, Bernard, and your August will meet someday, and you will need that little bluebird when the time comes. Keep it close to you. Remember the magic your father told you of the bluebird, and know that this one holds even more power than the story. It is a mulevi. It will make your deepest wish come true if only you will ask. But be careful how you use it, and don't use it frivolously. You will know beyond a shadow of a doubt when the time comes, and it will be the most powerful thing you will ever witness."

"What's a mulevi?"

"An item to reach the dead."

Savannah looked back and forth between the bluebird in her hand and the gypsy hobbling away. She wanted to tell the woman she didn't think she'd ever see August again, but she looked down at the bluebird and it gave her hope. Maybe August would come for her soon. When she looked back up, the woman was gone.

She remained on the bank and pondered the conversation for a long time. If the object was indeed a mulevi, maybe she could talk to her father. She really didn't understand the old woman or her cryptic messages, but she felt a new sense of encouragement for the future. She jumped up from the bank and ran all the way home. Maybe life would turn around very soon.

She ran up the stairs of her grandparent's house and sat down at the small writing desk in her room to write August a letter. She would give him every detail of the strange event. She began writing about the gypsy woman but couldn't find the words to describe her very well, so she crumpled up the piece of paper and threw it on the floor. She started a second time, relating that she thought her father knew this gypsy woman, but she crumpled that up and tossed it on the floor also. She made a third attempt, describing the glass bluebird, but that version too ended up in a ball on the floor. The words wouldn't come. They didn't make any sense. How was she supposed to explain any of this to August? Some gypsy woman gave her a magical bluebird, a mulevi? Should he keep his eyes open for some gypsy man named Bernard? And why? She thought about trying out a wish for her and August to be together, but the crone had told Savannah she would need the wish in the future, and she would know when to use it.

After hours of sitting at the desk, trying to put the strange event into words, and staring at the glass object, she gave up. She decided to tuck away the bluebird and forget about it for now. She slipped it into a small velvet-lined wooden box and placed the box in the back of her bureau drawer, covered with some clothing. She decided she wouldn't tell anyone. No one would believe her anyway. The more she thought about it, she wondered if she believed it herself. Magical bluebird. Pshaw.

As she stared at the ceiling that night, she allowed herself to hope that she'd be able to explain the whole encounter to August in person soon.

She always had this notion that August would come for her once he got a car. After hearing the gypsy woman's words, she expected him to appear at any moment. She didn't think the idea through, like what they would do once he got to New Orleans, but she knew deep in her heart he *would* come. She counted the days until his sixteenth birthday, allowing a few extra months for him to work and make some money to purchase a car.

When his sixteenth birthday and a few months had passed and he didn't arrive, she thought he would come for her when he was on summer break from school. He would certainly come see her then, even if it meant taking the train. She checked the train schedules, but he never appeared.

She then thought he would come for her after graduation, but he didn't. She hoped he would get a job and send for her, but he didn't get a job. She heard through some mutual friends that he received his undergrad degree and was now attending the Walter F. George School of Law in Atlanta. She soon understood why his letters were becoming further and further apart when she later heard he was dating a girl who lived in Atlanta.

Over the years, with each hope and disappointment, her heart felt like it broke into smaller and smaller pieces. With each passing week, month, season, year, she felt more and more alone. She moved through each day with a heavy heart and felt as if she would dry up and blow away if a strong enough wind came.

The wind came in the form of her high school graduation day. She walked onto the stage to receive her diploma, and saw her grandparents and Mary sitting with the other graduate's families. The grim looks on their faces told her everything she needed to know. Her mother had finally succumbed to the grief.

Three days later, Savannah stood by the grave,

holding Mary's hand. She never shed a tear.

By the time Savannah graduated from college herself, August had proposed marriage to the Atlanta girl and put a ring on her finger. Savannah received the devastating news about their engagement via a cut-out newspaper clipping sent from an old classmate. She locked herself in her room for an entire week, and she refused to speak with anyone for months. She had dreamt of August every night and planned their future every day since she moved to New Orleans, but August had moved on with his life. He had moved on without her. It took her a very long time to forgive him, even though she knew he never even realized he had hurt her. When his parents sent her a wedding invitation, she tore it up and retreated further into her private shell.

Through the years, both of Savannah's grandparents passed away. Mary married a young man named Billy and moved back to Biloxi. Mary said she wanted to raise her family in Biloxi, in the same lifestyle she and Savannah had loved so much. She planned to open a bakery and had invited Savannah to come back to Biloxi and help her, but Savannah didn't want to return to their childhood home. August and his new wife had moved back to Biloxi after he finished law school. Savannah didn't want to run into them and their new baby daughter in the small town.

She also didn't want to stay in New Orleans alone.

Chapter 6

Savannah turned her attention back to her kitchen and responded to her sister. "Thank you, Mary. I know Momma and Daddy loved August and would love to be here today. We sure have come full circle, haven't we? It was so hard leaving here after Daddy died, and even worse staying in Lakeview as long as we did. I would've never come back here if it hadn't been for you." Savannah's eyes started misting. She blinked the tears away and tried to smile. "Well, look where we are now—my wedding day—to August."

Mary smiled back as a tear rolled down her cheek.

Savannah gave her little sister a quick hug and then hustled out the front door with her purse in one hand and her car keys in the other. She put the top down on her brand new red Hudson Custom Eight convertible. I had been a gift from August, and though she could never imagine accepting such an extravagant gift in all her life, she couldn't resist the shiny new car. He went on and on about the speed and the foam seats and the great springs for a smooth ride. She had no idea what he was talking about. All she knew was she just loved the color.

She finished putting the top down, climbed into the driver's seat, and felt her shoulders relax a bit. She needed to feel the sun and the wind on her face today. She wanted to wash away the memories. She didn't know why she felt like running, but she didn't question it. It was a feeling she'd been familiar with most of her life. She'd wanted to run when Daddy died. She'd wanted to run when August didn't come for her. When depression and lithium took her mother, she'd wanted to run then, too. As long as she could remember, she always wanted to run away from life, but that would be impossible, wouldn't it? Strangely, she'd never given into the yearning. She'd always stayed put, perhaps paralyzed by fear—or pain.

Today, she could pretend she was running. She wanted to drive fast and let the wind blow these cobwebs out of her mind. She needed to let the rev of the engine drown out the old emotions. They were too much to deal with today, especially following the nightmare she woke from this morning. She glanced at her watch and frowned. She was running behind schedule. She had to focus on what needed to be done right now, today. She needed to put the old ghosts to rest.

She tied her scarf tight around her head, and the tires squealed as she pulled around the circular driveway and pressed the accelerator all the way down to the floor. She headed out to the street, passing rows and rows of weeping willows with their hanging Spanish moss. She sped through the gates, and the tires squealed again as she turned right onto Beach Road. She drove as fast as she could down the beachfront road, allowing the engine, the sun, the wind, and the roaring surf to ease her pain.

Chapter 7

August had a forty-minute leisurely drive to the office in Gulfport, which included a quick jaunt on the main thoroughfare through town for about ten minutes. His drive was always uneventful, often boring. He passed beautiful homes on the beachfront road, admired fishing boats in the gulf, and yielded for the occasional nanny pushing a carriage or a person walking a dog. As early in the morning as he left for work, usually the only traffic he saw was a milk truck or a school bus. His daughter, Emma, never took the bus. Emma's friends thought it beneath them to ride a bus and were driven to school in fancy cars, usually by a well-manicured mom or occasionally someone's chauffeur.

He didn't begrudge Emma anything. If she and her friends didn't want to ride the bus, then so be it. The child had lost her mother, and her father was never home, so the least he could give her was the freedom to not ride the school bus. The truth was, Emma had never known her mother, for she was only a few days old when Eula died following complications of the birth. Looking back, it seemed strange that Eula died of something like that. In the old days, women died in childbirth all the time, but not in this day and age. It still didn't make any sense to August. Emma was never told any specifics about her mother's death, but the girl seemed to be growing up with a chip on her shoulder and a sense of maturity well beyond her years. August noticed she always hesitated when people asked about her parents. She didn't like telling people she didn't have a mother, and because of that, she had very few friends and kept to herself. It was difficult to tell if she carried a sense of guilt for her mother's death or if she simply felt different because the other children all had mothers. Either way, August was determined to shower the girl with everything in his power to acquire. Love, presents, money, freedom. The only thing August couldn't give her was time. Becoming the newest partner at Burkhart, Young, Ryan, and Associates didn't come without its price. It was typical for August to work eighty or more hours a week. He wanted to spend more time with Emma, but as she was quickly growing up, she seemed less interested in spending more time with him. He was glad she was turning into an independent young woman, but sad that she didn't seem to need him at all. He tried not to dwell on the thought, as there wasn't much he could do about it. He was, however, immensely grateful Savannah had moved in with them. He couldn't have been more pleased with the way the girl's relationship was progressing. Emma and

Savannah were quickly becoming the best of friends, and August felt the weight of being a single parent melting off his shoulders.

Today, August's short drive to the office was unusual. As he pulled off Beach Road and onto the main road through town, traffic was unusually heavy, almost crawling, and he thought there must be an accident up ahead. He spent most of the time dead stopped, and twenty-five minutes into the ten-minute thoroughfare portion of his commute, he finally arrived at his street and stopped for gas. While the young attendant filled his tank, August ran inside the station to phone his office.

"Hi, Nancy, can you put Jimmy on the phone?" August asked his secretary.

"Certainly. One moment, Mr. Ryan."

Through the grimy window of the service station, he watched the attendant wash his windshield as he waited for Jimmy to pick up the phone.

"Hey, August, what time are you coming in?" Jimmy asked.

"Well, I thought I'd be there already, but there must be an accident in town or something. The traffic is at a complete standstill, but I just reached Walnut Street so I'm close. I have to make a quick stop at the store for a bottle of champagne so Savannah and I can have a private celebration tonight after the reception."

Jimmy chuckled. "That is so like you to try and get your date drunk. I'll tell you what, if that girl backs out, I'll marry you myself."

"You're not my type," August countered.

Jimmy laughed again, then said, "All right, buddy, get here as soon as you can. I'll wait until we're done with the paperwork before I go to lunch so I don't hold you up. See you in a bit."

"Sure thing. Bye, Jimmy." August hung up and went outside to pay the attendant.

He drove to the store a few blocks down Walnut Street and pulled into a front-row parking space. After chatting with Mr. Heath, the store owner, for a few moments, he spent a small fortune on the best bottle of champagne the store carried. When he returned to his car, he noticed it looked lopsided and immediately knew the reason. He walked around to the passenger side and found the back tire flat.

"Geez, I guess I'll get to work eventually. I could have already had this paperwork done by now."

Changing the tire was going to be a dirty job, but he didn't have any other options. He looked at the big clock on the bank tower across the street.

"It's 10:40? Oh, no, I better get moving." He took off his jacket and placed it and the champagne bottle on the passenger seat.

He walked to the front fender and removed the metal cover from the side mount, retrieved the spare tire, and rolled it around to the back.

Chapter 8

As Savannah pulled onto the thoroughfare, she couldn't believe how much traffic there was, and after sitting for twenty minutes in what seemed more a parking lot than a roadway, she decided she'd have to rearrange her schedule. She exited the thoroughfare and weaved back and forth across the narrow side streets on her way to the florist. It was a long distance out of the way, but anything was better than sitting in that traffic. The air was beginning to feel like a steam bath, with the sun beating down and the humidity rising swiftly, so when she reached the florist, she put the top back up on the car. She didn't want to show up sunburnt and wilted on her wedding day.

She entered the florist to the sound of a brass bell attached to the door and greeted the young woman behind the desk.

"Good morning, I'd like to pick up the flowers for the Ryan wedding, and I wonder if I could use your telephone."

The woman placed the phone on the reception counter and said she'd check on the flowers and would be right back.

Savannah dialed Sally's mom, Myrna, and fanned herself with her free hand as she waited for someone to pick up.

Emma and Sally had been best friends since elementary school, and the two frequently spent the night at each other's houses. Myrna didn't mind if they had sleepovers all the time, even on school nights, as long as they didn't stay up late. August never said anything about it one way or the other. He would let Emma have the moon if she wanted it.

"Hello?" Myrna answered.

"Hi, Myrna, it's Savannah."

"Oh, hi, Savannah. The girls are just finishing up breakfast. Did you want to speak with Emma?"

"No, I just wanted to tell you I'm running late. The traffic in town is stopped, and I sat in it for twenty minutes. I was going to pick up our flowers after I picked up Emma, but I decided to pick them up first. I'm at the florist now, so I hope you don't mind if I'm a little bit late."

"Not at all. I'm sure the girls can keep themselves occupied until you get here. You know how pre-teen girls are. They'll start putting on makeup and fixing their hair and changing clothes for the millionth time. I'll tell Emma you'll be here in a little while, okay?"

Savannah breathed a sigh of relief. "Thank you so much, Myrna. You're a lifesaver. Do me a favor and check the news and see if they say anything about that traffic in town. If it's something bad like an accident, maybe they'll mention it. I've had the radio on in the car, but I haven't heard anything."

"Oh, sure. I'll ring you back at the florist if I hear anything."

"All right, and I'll be at your house very soon."

Savannah hung up. She wondered if she should call the hair salon to change her eleven o'clock appointment. The clock on the wall behind the reception desk said it was already 10:40. She figured she and Emma would be only a few minutes late, so she decided to forego calling the salon and dialed August's office instead. She waited for the line to ring, but it never did. She tried a second time with the same result. She shrugged and hung up. "That is so strange," she muttered.

"Pardon me?" said the receptionist as she appeared again behind the desk.

"Oh, it's nothing. I was just trying to call someone, but the line seems to be dead."

She handed the telephone back to the young lady and asked if her flowers were ready. Savannah could see through the open doorway into the back room. There were two large waist-high tables covered in flowers, ribbons, and greenery, but she didn't see any boxes packed up.

Savannah wasn't a huge flower-store fan. She loved flowers and gardening, just not flower stores. Actually, they were often pleasant; what she didn't like was the flower-store smell. Even though many people found the aroma pleasing, it always smelled to her like a funeral.

"You seem to be a little early. We're finishing up the bouquet and centerpiece, so it'll be a few more minutes. Can I get you some coffee while you wait?"

"No, thank you. How long do you think it will be?"

"Maybe twenty minutes at the most. The corsages are finished. We're just working on the others. I'm sorry; we weren't expecting you until twelve. We'll get them boxed up as quickly as we can."

"That's okay. I don't mean to rush you." Savannah tried to be patient, though her heart was racing as she looked again at the clock on the wall. She faintly heard "Pennies from Heaven" by Bing Crosby playing on the radio in the back room. For some reason, the melody made her anxious. She felt like she was racing against time, as if the whole world was trying to make her late for her own wedding. She casually strolled around the store, admiring flower arrangements, and kept herself occupied glancing through some photographs in a book on the counter.

After a few minutes, the girl again checked the back room and returned to the counter. "Are you sure I can't get you some coffee?"

"No, really, I'm fine, but thank you." Savannah smiled. "Are they almost finished back there?"

"Yes, they have your bouquet boxed up and are working on the centerpiece."

"Can I go ahead and put the bouquet and corsages in my car while they finish?" Savannah asked.

"Sure," the girl replied. "Why don't you open up your car and I'll bring them out for you."

Savannah went out the front door to the jingle of the brass bell. The heat hit her like a hot oven and she grimaced. As she neared her car, she reached into her pocket for her car keys. They were not there. She didn't remember putting them in her purse, but she reached in there anyway. They weren't there, either. She tried the car door and found it locked. She turned her purse around to check the pocket on the opposite side. Not there. She tried the door handle again. Of course it was locked. That's how this day seemed to be going so far. How can she be locked out of the car when not ten minutes ago, she had the top down? She looked through the car's window, holding her hand above her eyes to block out the sun's glare. Her keys were right there—in the ignition.

Chapter 9

After changing the tire in the hot beating sun, August ran back into the store to buy a soda. He chugged an ice-cold bottle of RC Cola, thanked Mr. Heath, and returned to his car. He drove twice around his office building looking for a parking space before giving up and parking a couple blocks away. He had never seen traffic like this and didn't understand what was going on. As he neared the building, arriving an hour and a half later than he had planned, he noticed a news reporter on the sidewalk asking questions of passersby. The man wore a gray fedora with a small, square sign that read "Press" stuck in the band, and he held the stump of an unlit cigar between his fingers. August had seen this man many times before. With the county offices located in the building, it wasn't unusual for that reporter to loiter on the sidewalk, waiting for someone, anyone, to give him a quote. August figured he was probably asking questions about the upcoming court hearing and the location of the proposed golf course. Being on the litigating team, August wasn't at liberty to discuss the case before Monday's court date, so he put his head down and walked fast to avoid the man and his questions.

August's law office was on the top floor of a six-story Victorian building located in the center of town. On the first floor of the building sat a cafe, a gift shop, and a small accountant's office. The second and third floors were filled with various small businesses, and the fourth and fifth floors housed the city offices. Since this was the upscale part of town and the ornate building housed the mayor and the county's board of directors, the building also sported a red-carpeted entry and a doorman—an elderly black gentleman with salt-and-pepper hair, dressed in a red coat and a black top hat. Everyone called him Duke. August didn't know if that was the man's real name, but he did know Duke would be there every day, just as he had been for the last thirteen years, rain or shine, to greet August warmly.

"Good morning, Mr. Ryan." Duke smiled as he grabbed the large brass handle of the front door and pulled it open.

"Good morning, Duke."

"Congratulations on your upcoming wedding, sir. Please give your lovely bride my regards."

"I certainly will. Thank you very much," August responded with a smile.

"You are very welcome, sir. Have a nice day," Duke said as he closed the door.

August took the elevator to the sixth floor and emerged into his busy office. A huge maple reception desk rested on a white marble floor outside the elevator door, and behind it stood a partition which read *Burkhart, Young, Ryan, and Associates* in gold letters. There were expensive chairs and fancy tables to his right and left in front of more partitions. Sitting at the desk was a smart-looking young woman who was the receptionist for the entire law office.

"Good morning, Mr. Ryan," she said as he stepped off the elevator.

"Good morning, Miss Berry."

He turned left, rounded the corner into his private office, and saw Nancy at her desk outside his door. He handed her the bottle of champagne and asked her to put it on ice and to make sure he didn't forget it when he left.

Nancy was a very attractive brunette, with her hair cut in a smart bob and black-rimmed glasses that made her look like a schoolmarm. She took the bottle and glanced at August's dirty shirt and hands, but she said nothing. That was precisely why August thought the world of her. She seemed to know everything that was going on without ever asking any questions, and she always gave give him exactly what he needed without being asked.

"I'll let Jimmy know you're here, and I'll bring you a clean shirt," Nancy said.

What would August do without her? She was a godsend.

August hadn't even reached his desk chair when Nancy entered behind him with a fresh shirt and placed it on the hook inside the door of his private restroom. When one worked regularly with judges and important people like the mayor, one kept a few clean shirts and ties in the office, just in case.

"Jimmy will be here in a moment," she said.

August glanced out the window and saw a lot of people milling around on the street in front of the building. He turned to ask Nancy if she knew what was going on outside, but she was already gone. He washed his hands and face and changed his shirt. He then sat down behind his desk and was looking through his mail when Jimmy knocked and opened the door.

"Hiya, groom," said Jimmy as he barged into the office.

August and Jimmy had been friends for years, and August was comfortable with Jimmy's boundless energy and his habit of barging in. When August was a senior in high school, Jimmy had entered the school as a freshman. He was a thin, scrawny boy who didn't know how to stave off the older, bigger boys who wanted to show off their masculinity to the girls. August stepped in when Jimmy was getting his lights knocked out by some bullies, and since that day, it seemed Jimmy had been paying August back. On occasion, August even thought Jimmy went into law so they could remain friends.

"Hi, Jimmy, what's up? Sorry I'm running so late. Do you have the paperwork we need to go over?" August asked.

"Yup, got it right here." He patted the thick folder he held in his hand. "The county board wants this over and done with right away. They're getting anxious about getting those gypsies off the land so they can start building. And the mayor is breathing down their necks, so nothing can go wrong with this. What took you so long to get here? Were you stuck in traffic all this time?"

"No. First I was stuck in traffic, and then I changed a flat tire."

"A flat? You sure picked a good day to have bad traffic and a flat tire," teased Jimmy. "Well, let's get to work here. We all have a wedding to go to after lunch and you're holding us up."

Jimmy spread the papers out on the small conference table at the far end of August's office.

As August grabbed a few pens and headed toward the table, Nancy rapped on the door and stuck her head in. "Would you gentlemen like coffee or anything?"

"Yeah, coffee would be great, Nancy. Thank you," August replied.

A few minutes later, Nancy brought them a fresh pot and set up a coffee service on the lacquered European chest behind the conference table, complete with linen napkins and silver spoons.

August sipped hot coffee as he looked down at the papers with his brow furrowed. "Why can't the city planners simply move the golf course down the beach a few hundred yards? Why do they have to uproot these people?"

"Because the mayor's brother is one of the primary investors and he's calling the shots. They're building the course to entertain clients, and they don't want those vagabonds anywhere near their high-end clientele."

"They're not vagabonds, Jimmy. They're gypsies."

"I don't see the difference. They don't have homes. They're bums."

"No, bums beg for handouts and annoy people."

"Okay, so they're not bums because they don't beg. But there are rumors that they're thieves."

"If they were thieves, we would be prosecuting them or defending them. Not one of them has ever been in our offices. We've never had any problem with them. Moving them off their land by force is just wrong."

"It's not their land. They've set up a wagon village on public property—property the mayor and his cronies want to build a golf course on—so they have to go."

August shook his head. "Sometimes being on the right side of the law doesn't feel like it's the right side."

"I know, but this paperwork needs to get finished so we can present the case in court on Monday. The judge will evict them, and the matter will be settled once and for all."

"And where are they supposed to go? They came up here from New Orleans after getting kicked out of there to make room for a railroad. Why can't they be left alone? How many times do these poor people have to be evicted?"

"At least once more."

Chapter 10

His mother always warned him about the gajo, or white man. She told him the gajo don't like the gypsies and always ran them out of everyplace they have ever lived, so she told him to keep his head down and mind his own business. He wasn't very good at doing either. He was a hot-tempered child who grew up to be a hot-tempered man.

"Bernard, no matter what happens, you will never be accepted as white. You need to always stay true to your gypsy heritage."

He took that as a direct order and used it as permission to push his agenda with the gajo at every opportunity, often getting into fistfights following late-night saloon visits and brawls in town for no reason. The white people would never understand the gypsy ways or culture, and they would never like the gypsies, so he didn't see a problem with taking a swing every now and then.

"I can see your future, Bernard," his mother told him. "I know the conflict you will face against the gajo. But you are half white, so you must find a way other than your fists to win the battle. You've always been such a hot-headed boy. Maybe you should reason with them, try to get them to see the error of their ways without losing your temper. Your anger will only lead you down a bad road. The battle I speak of will occur long after I'm gone, so I won't be here to help you."

"Don't speak like that, Mother. Of course you'll be here."

She sipped her coffee and let him sit in silence as he looked off down the beach. Finally, he broke the stillness. "What about my father?"

"He is gone already." A dark cloud filled her eyes and her expression grew sad.

"Tell me about him, Mother."

She looked into his eyes. "I'll tell you one thing. He was one of the gajos who ran us out of New Orleans with his railroad. It was just after you were born. I tried to make friends with him and get him to see our plight, but I made a grave mistake and fell in love with him. I was young; I was stupid. I certainly wasn't as wise as I am now. I lost him because of my own magic. I thought I could change the future I saw, but I only made it happen more quickly." She looked off across the water and wrinkled her forehead at the memory. After a moment, she turned back to him and reached over and patted his hand. "But I have you, so it was meant to be, wasn't it?"

Chapter 11

After an hour or so, August and Jimmy finished their task. Jimmy stacked up the mountain of papers and said he would ask Nancy to send them to the senior partner's office. August sat on the corner of his desk and picked up the telephone to call Savannah. He hadn't dialed the first number yet when Nancy flew into the office, her brow furrowed. She never came in without knocking. Ever. August stopped dialing, finger in midair, and looked at her. "Is something wrong, Nancy?"

"Yes, Mr. Ryan, I think there is. A police officer just came up the elevator and demanded we lock ourselves in our offices. He said there is a man with a gun in the building." She was out of breath and her cheeks were flushed.

"A man with a gun? What man? Where?" August dropped the phone back into its cradle and rose to his feet.

"I don't know. The officer just said we have to stay put and that the elevator is off limits. We have to stay in our offices until further notice," she replied, wringing her hands.

Jimmy was moving toward the radio as Nancy was talking. He turned it on and dialed in the local news station. They could barely hear the anchor through the static, and Jimmy adjusted the antenna to try to bring the voice in more clearly. The anchor said a police situation had been brewing all morning. A gypsy man had attacked a local gun shop owner and stolen a shotgun, and though the shop owner would recover, the police had the local roads closed while they searched for the suspect. He was recently spotted near or in the mayor's office building and the news station was trying to reach a reporter who was already near the scene. The public was being asked for help spotting the gypsy man, described as about thirty years old with a heavy beard and long, bushy brown hair. The anchor reiterated that this man was armed and dangerous, and anyone who saw him should call the police department and not approach him. The anchor said the station would have more news as events unfolded.

August, Nancy, and Jimmy were frozen as they stared at the radio. The news went to a commercial for *The Great Ziegfeld* before any of them moved or breathed.

August picked up the telephone and hung it up again as he stared at the radio. He couldn't call Savannah now. This would only worry her. He hoped she was on the road or at the salon and wasn't listening to the news.

"Oh, come on," August said under his breath.

"I have to find a way to get out of this building." He looked at his gold watch. "It's almost noon. I have to get to the church. They can't demand that we sit here all day. Maybe I can sneak down the stairs, cut through the cafe's kitchen, and go out the back door into the alley. Nancy, do you think there are policemen in the back alley? Or are they all in the building?"

"I don't know how many there are or where they are, Mr. Ryan. Oh, dear. I hope they catch this person quickly."

Chapter 12

Savannah exchanged pleasantries with Myrna and Sally and hustled Emma out to the car. They were supposed to be at the hair salon at eleven. Due to taking the back roads through town and the long wait for the man from the service station to come and unlock her car, it was already noon.

"So, did you have a nice sleepover?" Savannah asked as she pulled out of Sally's driveway.

"Sure. I always have fun with Sally. We spent most of the time trying to recreate clothes from her mom's fashion magazines. Which reminds me, when are we going shopping for school clothes? School starts next week."

Emma was always ahead of everyone else. She knew dates and times and appointments in advance. Savannah thought Emma must have inherited that attention to detail from her mother, and Savannah wished she could borrow that talent for a few days, so she wouldn't forget things like picking up dog food. Out of the corner of her eye, Savannah saw Emma staring at her, awaiting an answer.

"Oh, boy." Savannah shook her head like something inside was loose. "With all the planning for the wedding, I totally lost track of time. I guess school is coming up fast, huh? We'll have to go shopping as soon as your dad and I get back from our honeymoon."

"Well, what I was thinking"—Emma looked down at the floorboard—"is that if you could just give me the money for the clothes, I could go shopping at the department store with Sally while you're away. That way, when you come home, there will be nothing for you to do. What do you think of that plan?"

Savannah thought August might not like the idea very much, though she didn't have a problem with it herself.

"Well?" Emma said. "What do you think?"

"I think that would be a fine idea. As long as you know that it's not because I don't want to take you shopping." Savannah paused for a moment before continuing. "We just have to find a way to convince your dad that you're old enough to pick out your own school clothes and you won't go to school looking like a Chicago flapper. But don't you worry about it. I'll think of something."

She glanced over at Emma and smiled. She had only been in Emma's life for a little over a year, but had observed an already mature adolescent blossoming into a fine young woman. She loved Emma with all her heart, and, just like Emma's dad, could never bring herself to say no to the girl.

"Okay," Savannah continued, "we need to hurry and get to the beauty salon. We were supposed to get our hair done at eleven."

They arrived at the salon and were rushed to their respective stations. They chatted with the beauticians, talking about the wedding and the upcoming school year. After sitting in the chairs for a long time, Savannah and Emma had gentle curls around their faces. They admired their hairdos in the large mirrors, to the oohs and ahhs of the ladies in the salon.

"My goodness, it's 1:00," Savannah said to Emma as she paid the receptionist at the front desk. "We'd better get home and get dressed. We don't want to be late today, do we?" She asked the receptionist if she could quickly use the phone to call her sister and let her know they were on their way. After a few rings, Mary answered.

"Hi, Mary," Savannah said, digging into her purse for her car keys.

"Hi, Savvy. Everything okay?"

"Yes, we've been running unbelievably behind all day, and I had to call the service station to unlock my car because I locked my keys in the ignition. Can you believe that? But we now have the flowers and our hair done, and we're headed home to get dressed."

"Good," said Mary. "Boomer is all bathed and groomed, and we'll keep him here for the night. Billy and I are dressed and are about to head to your house right now. Do you need us to pick anything up on the way?"

"Nope, we're good. We'll see you there in about forty minutes or so, as long as that traffic in town has cleared up," said Savannah.

"I heard there's something going on, but I didn't catch what it was. The police have a couple roads blocked or something. Take the back roads so you don't run into traffic. I'll have Billy get the flowers out of your car and put them in ours when you get there."

They hung up.

Emma said, "I love Aunt Mary. She reminds me of you sometimes. Are she and Uncle Billy going to have children someday? I'd love to have a little cousin to play with. Maybe they'd even let me babysit for them."

"I guess they will someday. They moved back here from New Orleans because they thought it would be a great place to raise a family, but Aunt Mary has been so busy with her bakery, it seems as though children may have been put off for a little while," Savannah explained as she dialed August's office.

Again, the line was dead.

"I just can't reach your father today. The phone lines haven't been working all day." Savannah frowned. "Well, I hope he's on his way."

They pulled onto the side street and headed toward Beach Road.

Chapter 13

The trio listened to the radio but received no further updates. August paced the floor like a caged animal. Jimmy cracked open the office door and didn't see anyone in the outer office, so he tiptoed behind Nancy's desk and cracked open the stairwell door. He stood silently with the door open an inch and listened for voices. No voices, no footsteps. He returned to August's office.

"What does it look like?" August asked.

"I don't see anybody. I think you can get down the stairwell like you said."

August placed a gentle hand on Nancy's shoulder and told her to stay put in his office until the police said it was safe to come out. He grabbed his suit coat, inched open his office door, and stepped into the outer office. At that very moment, the ding of the elevator sounded and a police officer emerged and spotted him between the partitions.

"Please go back into your office and close the door, sir. The suspect is loose in the building."

August backed up a foot toward his office. "Loose in the building?"

"Yes, sir."

Just then, the stairwell door flew open. A crazed man bolted out of the stairwell and stopped when he saw August. The man looked around wildly, but with the partition at his back, he didn't see the policeman standing on the other side. The man was dressed in dirty trousers and a wrinkled shirt with stains on the front. His beard hung long, as well as his hair. August instantly knew the man was the gypsy the police were looking for.

The officer stood on the other side of the partition, out of the man's line of sight, but the officer saw the surprised look on August's face. He pulled his gun and swiftly rounded the corner.

"*Freeze!*" the officer yelled.

The man pulled his gun from behind his back and waved it wildly in the air.

A woman screamed at the far end of the hall and the man looked in that direction. He ran toward the voice, passing Nancy's desk, and running right between the police officer and August.

"*FREEZE!*" the officer yelled again.

Shots were fired, followed by more screams.

And it was over as fast as it had begun.

The gunman lay on the floor, unmoving, in front of Nancy's desk, blood staining his shirt from the wound in his chest. It had also splattered on the rug, turning it from soft beige to a spotted burgundy. The officer cautiously approached with his gun still aimed at the man. He kicked the man's gun from his hand, patted him down for any other weapons, pulled his wallet from his pocket, and flipped it open. Then he grabbed the telephone from Nancy's desk.

"The suspect is down on the sixth floor. Repeat, the suspect has been shot and is down on the sixth floor." He read from the man's wallet. "His name is Bernard Corning."

August recognized the name. The man was one of those gypsies from the beach who had been in the paper recently trying to gain sympathy for the gypsies and rally against the golf course. August remembered something about the man living alone since he had no parents or wife or children.

August knew this happened because of the proposed golf course location and the gypsy camp, but he didn't know if the man was aiming for someone in his law office or someone in the mayor's office. Either way, he was glad it was over. He felt sorry for the gypsies, and certainly felt bad for the now deceased Bernard Corning. The gypsies had never caused any trouble in the community other than minor drunken skirmishes, and August wondered if the coming hearing made this man go crazy, or if he was already crazy before. A man dying for something as insignificant as the location of a golf course seemed so wrong.

August glanced around the office at his stunned coworkers who were slowly emerging from their offices to see what had happened. Other police officers were undoubtedly on their way up to the sixth floor, and if he was going to get out of there, it would have to be now. He slowly stepped sideways toward the stairwell and silently cracked open the door. He listened for footsteps on the stairs but heard none.

He entered the stairwell, ran down six flights of stairs, cut through the café kitchen, and left the building through the alley without being seen.

Chapter 14

It was a hot summer night, the humidity hanging over downtown New Orleans like a wet blanket. Thomas Blakely had been working in the sun all day and wanted nothing more than a cold drink and a place to sit down and relax. He found most of the local watering holes too noisy, and ended up at a quiet little hole in the wall down by the beach with a hand-painted sign out front that read Kertsheema.

"What can I getcha?" the shapely redhead approached him.

"Just a beer. Whatever you have that's cold and wet." He smiled at her and admired her sexy figure, clothed in a tight, white low-cut blouse and long skirt. He loved how her ringlets fell around her face as she looked down to pour his beer.

She slopped the cold mug on the counter in front of him. "You one of those railroad workers?"

"Yes, I am. I've been here about two months overseeing the repair of the track. Apparently it was destroyed by some gypsies."

"Yeah, I think I've seen you around a couple times." She pulled a rag out of her apron and wiped down the bar. "Maybe the gypsies had a reason to destroy the track."

He sipped his beer and sighed when the cold liquid hit the back of his throat. "Maybe they should stay away from property that doesn't belong to them," he fired back. "If my company finds out who did it, there will certainly be consequences."

"Consequences, huh? Well, I might know something about it, not that I would ever tell. We're a tight community around here."

He looked around the small, dank room. It was filled with old, decrepit tables and worn chairs. The walls looked like someone had slapped up a few pieces of plywood and then covered the roof with the same. He doubted the building could withstand a rain shower, much less the strong storms that regularly howled in across the lake. He guessed the place had to be rebuilt at least three or four times a year, but at least the beer was cold. Only a handful of people were there, and they all seemed to be eyeing him, which he found a little unnerving.

"Are you Kertsheema?" he asked the barmaid.

She laughed. "No, Kertsheema means tavern."

"Oh, I'm sorry. Well, what's your name?"

"Salina. Salina Corning. And yours?"

"Thomas Blakely."

She wiped her hand on the towel and held it out to him. "It's nice to meet you Thomas Blakely."

After a few moments of awkward silence, he asked, "Why is it so quiet around here when every other place on the waterfront is packed tonight?"

"People like you don't generally come around these parts."

"What do you mean, people like me?"

"Gajos. You know, white people. Gajos don't usually mingle with gypsies."

"Gypsies? This is a gypsy place?" He looked around again at the patrons and then back at Salina. "Are you a gypsy?"

"Yes, sir, born and raised." She winked at him.

He cocked his head and looked at her. She was beautiful, certainly not the image of an old gypsy hag he had embedded in his head.

She smiled again, seductively this time, and offered to refill his beer.

After a few hours of chatting and countless refills of beer—and maybe a few shots of whiskey; he couldn't remember—Salina closed the bar and walked with Thomas down the beach in the moonlight. He stopped and faced the lake. The cool evening breeze felt good on his sunburnt face. He longed to remove his shirt and feel it caress his red shoulders.

As if Salina could read his mind, she stepped in front of him and began to unbutton his shirt. He looked down and staggered a bit as he watched her fingers move expertly on his buttons. He thought she said she had a feeling he'd come here one day, but that didn't make sense, so he must have misheard her under the lapping of the waves and the wind in his ears. The feeling of her soft hands on his bare chest removed any remaining rational thoughts from his head. She rose on her toes and kissed him on the mouth. The taste of her was intoxicating. They lowered themselves onto the ground and he allowed her to seduce him on the powdery soft sand.

In the afterglow, she rested her head on his chest and he thought he heard her say, "I've been waiting for you for the last few months. I'm glad you're finally here." He didn't hear her clearly as he had started to doze off, but the sound of her voice brought him back to reality. Abruptly, he rose and started to button his pants, weaving back and forth and mumbling that what just happened was a big mistake.

"Salina, I'm sorry, but I have a girl in town."

She rolled over on her back and looked up at him with no expression.

"Her name is Gertrude," he continued as he bent over to pick up his shirt and stumbled a bit.

She sat up and pulled her white blouse over her tan shoulders, smiling up at him in a way that suggested she could make him forget about all other girls. He was fairly certain she was correct.

He shook the sand out of his shirt before putting it on.

"I'm sorry, Salina," he slurred, "but I have to go. Please allow me to walk you home." He offered his hand to help her rise. She accepted the offer and never took her eyes off his face.

Gawd, she was stunning!

While they walked, with her arm entwined around his, and him reluctantly allowing it, she told him a magical story about a bluebird.

The next morning he woke with an aching head and a foggy memory of a redheaded gypsy woman on the beach. He wondered which parts of the evening's events were real and which were a liquor-induced dream. It was all a hazy web of desire and guilt. Through his pounding headache, he vowed to never drink again.

That afternoon, he picked up Gertrude from her house, and while they were walking through the park, Gertrude pointed out a tiny bluebird. The previous evening's events came rushing back to him. He still didn't remember all the details, but he remembered the woman telling him the story of the bluebird and how it was a sign of love. He asked Gertrude to marry him at that very moment, and he never saw Salina again.

Chapter 15

By the time Savannah and Emma pulled into the driveway, Savannah realized she was smiling. The time for the wedding was near and she was beginning to feel the excitement. She was deep in thought, remembering their childhood, trying to forget the pain of living without August for so many years, and imagining how wonderful this evening was going to be. If it turned out anything like the day she and August got engaged, it would be perfect.

They had enjoyed a most scrumptious supper at a fancy seafood restaurant by the pier. They dined on oysters and shrimp and drank champagne until they were heady and giddy. At one point a photographer offered to take their picture. Savannah shook her head, but August insisted on having their photograph taken. He gave the photographer some money and his office address and asked that the photograph be delivered.

Following supper, they walked outside onto the deck to view the summer sky in the balmy night air. The moon was full, shining a path of white on the ocean, and the breeze was gentle and warm. August asked Savannah if she would like to go for a walk down the beach and she consented. They walked down the wooden steps to the powder-like sand, kicked off their shoes, and strolled hand in hand along the moonlit surf.

After a few minutes of walking, August stopped and turned to face the water.

"What are you looking at?" Savannah asked.

"I'm just thinking how big this world is and how lucky I am to have someone to share it with." August squeezed her hand.

He paused for a long moment before continuing. "I've been alone for a long time. It's been very difficult. Not only to raise a child by myself, but to go to bed every night with no one to talk to or hold. After Emma's mom died, I poured myself into my work. I got through each day by ignoring life. Time passed, but I don't know how, and I must admit I don't remember most of it. I thought about you all the time, wondering where you were and what you were doing. I don't know how we ever lost each other in the first place." He faced Savannah and took her hands in his. "But, since we've been reunited, Emma has been happier, I made partner at the firm, I have beautiful gardens that you created…heck, I even have a dog." He laughed awkwardly. "My dreary house has become a home. My empty life is now filled with a real family—all because of you."

August reached into his pocket and pulled out a small black box. He opened it as he knelt on one knee in the sand.

"I've loved you since we were children. I will love you when we're old and gray. I will love you forever, for all eternity. I don't ever want to lose you again, Savannah. Will you marry me?"

Savannah's heart beat so fast, she thought it would burst. She felt a tear roll down her cheek. She had waited for this moment her entire life.

She, too, had spent long years moving mindlessly from day to day without ever really feeling like she was living. She would now have a family, a stepdaughter, a beautiful home, and August. Yes, she would finally have August. Years ago, she'd climbed onto a train and looked hopelessly out the window as it chugged away, and she hoped someday, somehow, some way, she and August would be together again. Now it was all coming true.

"Yes," was the only word she could muster.

August took the ring out of the box and placed it on her finger. Then he stood up and took her in his arms and melted her with the sweetest kiss any woman had ever known. They were silent for a long time, looking out across the moonlit water with their arms wrapped around each other.

"I am the happiest man in the world," August said.

Savannah squeezed her arms around his waist, leaned her head onto his shoulder, and smiled. She thought this must be a dream, and she did not want the sound of her own voice to wake her from it.

As they walked back to the car, August asked, "So, when would you like to get married?"

"As soon as possible."

Chapter 16

The sun was beginning to set, and the sky was rippled with watercolor shades of red, pink, and yellow. The evening breeze was so gentle, it was almost like a butterfly kissing one's skin. The cobblestone patio was decorated with a multitude of candles, and the garden flowers not only looked beautiful in the moonlight, but filled the air with the scent of sweet autumn clematis vines. A small waterfall babbled into a lily pond, where patches of white and yellow flowers floated.

A cobblestone walkway ran down the length of the country club, with a couple sets of french doors lining the stone wall. Radiating through the open doors were tantalizing aromas of roasted duck, walnut salad, and spiced pumpkin cake. Inside, the orchestra's music mixed with the muted sound of the crowd's voices and the clinking of silver touching china. Occasionally, there was a laugh above the din, and less frequently, the sound of a loon could be heard from the direction of the pond. The weather, the moon, the entire evening could not have been more perfect. August appeared on the patio, pulling Savannah through one of the french doors, away from the crowd of friends and family.

"Mrs. Ryan, I have never seen you look more ravishing," he said as he spun her around in her wedding gown.

Savannah's dress billowed like a cloud as she moved, and the glimmering beads, hand sewn into the bodice, glittered like diamonds in the patio's candlelight.

"Indeed, you sparkle like a rare diamond," August continued.

She smiled back at him.

The orchestra began to play "Stardust" and August led Savannah to one of the alcoves. He took her in his arms and kissed her on the forehead. They danced alone without saying a word. As the music reached a crescendo, August released his hold from her waist and spun her around again. He didn't notice the waterfall in the lily pond had splashed water onto the alcove, making the cobblestones wet. He didn't know Savannah's new wedding shoes would be slippery on the wet stones. He didn't realize what had happened until Savannah was lying on the ground.

"Savannah! Savannah! Are you okay?" August fell to his knees next to her.

Savannah didn't answer. August shook her, but she didn't respond.

"Savannah?"

He then noticed Savannah's head was lying on the stone edging that stood about four inches higher that the rest of the cobblestones, and he realized she must have hit her head when she slipped and fell.

"*Savannah!*" August lifted her limp torso and rested her head on his lap. He touched her face and called her name again and again. He reached his hand around the back of her head and felt something wet. He held his hand up to look at it, and even in the dim light could see his hand covered with blood.

Behind him, he heard someone scream and a woman yell, "Someone call a doctor!"

Chapter 17

The sky was gray and overcast, matching everyone's mood. A storm was brewing out in the gulf and the newsman said it would probably rain most of the afternoon. Not a heavy downpour until late at night, but assuredly a constant drizzle throughout the day.

Duke, in a pressed black doorman jacket, stood like a statue in front of August's home as expensive cars pulled into the driveway and black overcoats and umbrellas emerged from them and entered the house. Duke greeted everyone formally, opening and closing the large wooden door for them. Nancy was in the front parlor, greeting guests and taking everyone's umbrellas, hats, coats, and envelopes with cards and condolence messages.

The house smelled of flowers, some of which had been delivered, some brought back from the church. The funeral had lasted more than three hours.

The service was held at Fisherman's Church, after which the guests had driven all the way out to Biloxi City Cemetery. They now came to the house for the wake, which Nancy had planned. The guests filed into the kitchen, where the girls from Mary's bakery were helping out, making sandwiches and filling coffee cups.

Emma sat at the dining table in a formal black cotton dress, pushing a tuna salad sandwich around on a plate. She hadn't eaten a bite of it. Grown-ups patted her on the head or the shoulder as they walked by, but very few said more than the required, "I'm very sorry, Emma," to her.

Boomer scratched on the back door. Emma took her sandwich and opened the door an inch. That way she could speak to Boomer but he couldn't squeeze in. "No, Boomer, you have to stay outside until these people leave," she whispered.

He cocked his head and whined. She gave him the sandwich. He gobbled it in one bite and looked up at her for more. He was soaking wet from the constant drizzle, but there was nothing she could do for him. She closed the door and sat back down at the table.

Mary and Billy entered the kitchen and sat down with her.

"Emma, would you like to come stay with us for a few days? We would love to have you come visit," Mary said.

Emma looked at her for a moment before finally saying, "No, thank you."

"Well, if you change your mind, the offer is always open. You can bring Boomer and stay as long as you want. This house might be too busy for a little while. If you need a break, you call me, and I'll run over and pick you up."

Emma nodded and looked back down at her now empty plate.

Mary shrugged at Billy, and they both got up from the table and went into the living room to greet guests.

Boomer again scratched softly on the door. Emma looked at him through the glass and shook her head. She stared at her plate for a while longer and finally rose from the table, grabbed a wide-brimmed hat from the hook inside the pantry, and went outside. Boomer followed her through the drizzle, past the drenched and sagging flower garden, to the tree swing on the side of the yard, where they stayed for the rest of the afternoon.

When afternoon turned to evening, the guests started leaving. Emma watched their cars pulling down the drive, and then she headed back inside and went up the stairs to get ready for bed. It had been such a long day, and she was so utterly miserable and tired. As she crawled into bed, she heard Boomer bark outside. She ran down the stairs and into the kitchen to open the door for him.

There had been a break in the rain. She wondered if it would rain again tomorrow or if the break would last, but she really didn't care if it rained forever. She opened the glass door and saw Boomer staring at the tree swing, wagging his tail and barking. Emma called his name and he looked at her, then back out at the swing. "No, I'm not coming back out to the swing. Come inside." She couldn't see anything in the dark back yard and figured a raccoon or something must be rooting around by the swing. She told Boomer a second time to come inside, but he seemed more interested in barking at the swing. Finally, with the promise of a treat, she convinced the silly dog to come in.

After he devoured his treat, he followed her upstairs and plopped down at the foot of her bed. They both fell into a fitful sleep.

Chapter 18

Later that night, August stood on the back porch staring into the darkness of the yard. The sky was muted by shades of black and gray and the flower gardens were nothing but shadows. The wind had stopped. The air was deathly still. This was the calm before the mighty storm that was surely heading their way. On the left side of the yard, next to the enormous oak that held the swing, were a couple of small apple trees Savannah had planted the year before. Scattered across the yard were half a dozen flower beds, also containing bushes and large stones, and in the middle of the largest flower bed rested a bench and small bath for the birds that Boomer liked to chase away. At the far end of the yard on the right side stood a gazebo. It was actually only the frame of a gazebo. August was supposed to finish it last spring but he never got around to it. From this angle, in the darkness, it looked finished.

"The clouds must be playing tricks on my eyes," August whispered to himself. "Things always look different in the darkness," he then said out loud, because the sound of his own whisper gave him a shiver.

Out of the corner of his eye, he saw something move in the center garden, near the birdbath. At first, he thought it was Boomer, but quickly remembered he had heard the dog go upstairs with Emma. August remained still and squinted into the darkness, but he saw nothing. He glanced at the gazebo to his right and then the swing to his left. He froze. There was no wind at all, but the tree swing was swaying back and forth all by itself.

Chapter 19

The torrential downpours had lasted an entire week, but today, the weather had almost magically transformed into a crisp and sunny day. Mary arrived at the house to pick up Emma to go shopping. With all that had happened, everyone seemed to have forgotten that school had started and Emma needed clothes and supplies. Mary had called Emma and offered to take her shopping, and Emma had reluctantly agreed. The poor girl was not looking forward to the school year, but was more than ready to get out of the house for a little while, away from the depression that now lived there.

August sat on the back porch in the rays of the warm sunshine, staring off into the garden. That seemed to be all he did anymore. It confused him that life seemed to go on in plants and flowers, but he couldn't seem to make it happen for himself. He didn't go to work, he didn't speak to anyone, he didn't leave the house, he didn't even shower. He just sat in the yard. The flowers were dying off in the fall coolness, and he understood the pain they must feel every year when summer comes to an end.

Boomer walked up to him and barked. August petted him on the head and looked around the patio. He realized he hadn't closed the glass door. *Why is it so hard to get it together?* he thought. Boomer wagged his tail and bounced down the patio steps, running off into the garden to chase a bird out of the bath.

The more August thought about what had happened, the more angry he became. He seemed to wobble between sadness and anger at every moment. As controlling as he was with every aspect of his life, he couldn't control his mood swings, which made him even more furious.

He followed Boomer down the steps into the garden. He stood next to the large flower bed and stared down at the dying flowers and the mud left over from the storm. His eyes filled with blinding tears, and he fell to his knees. He couldn't make sense of what had happened and he felt the world crashing around him. They had their whole lives ahead of them. Now everything was gone. His Savannah was gone.

He grabbed a handful of flowers, ripped them from the soil, and threw them across the yard. He reached out for another handful. He ripped up every single flower he could get his hands on, yanking them up by the roots and throwing them over his shoulder. He cried and pulled and pulled and cried, and when his tantrum was over, he sat in the grass and sobbed for a long, long time. The sobs tore from his chest like they were tearing directly from his soul.

When the wave of grief finally subsided and his tears ended, he looked around at what was left of the garden. He had demolished the one thing Savannah had treasured so much, which made him feel even worse. Savannah had spent so much time creating beauty, and he had destroyed it in a rage he couldn't control. In frustration, he reached up and pushed over the birdbath, splashing water all over the muddy mess he had created.

Chapter 20

Boomer ran into the house through the open glass door and bounced into the kitchen. He suddenly stopped in the middle of the room, looked down the hall, and cocked his head as if he had heard something. He bounded down the hallway and pushed open the door of the den with his nose. He wagged his tail furiously as he approached the overstuffed leather chair. He had been trained that he'd only be petted if he sat down, so he sat and waited. She reached down and patted his head.

Savannah emerged from the study with Boomer tagging along beside her. They entered the kitchen and she went into the pantry to get him a treat. While he ate it, she noticed the glass door was open, so she walked over and closed it. She stood at the doorway and looked into the yard and saw mud everywhere. All of her flowers had been pulled up from their roots, and the birdbath was lying on its side.

"Oh, no." She shook her head in disbelief and sadness. The flowers were no big deal. Boomer had dug up her flowers many times before, and they were done blooming for the season anyway, but she didn't think she could take the pain of losing one more thing. She breathed deeply, trying to push down the grief, and she turned to Boomer. He wagged his tail and panted in a way that made him look like he was smiling. She sighed. "Boomer, why are you such a bad dog?"

She then turned back to the door and looked out into the horizon and whispered, "August, I wish you could hear me. I love you and miss you so much."

✳✳✳

August sat on the grass on the far side of the large flower bed, shocked and saddened by the mess he'd made. Mud and plants were scattered all over the grass and on the overturned birdbath. He thought it a good thing the bushes at his back were too large for him to pull out of the dirt, because he would have destroyed those, too.

As he tried to compose himself, he recognized how grateful he was that Emma was shopping with Mary and wasn't home to witness his meltdown. He closed his eyes and concentrated on his breathing. Again and again, he breathed in slowly through his nose, pursed his lips and exhaled. He stopped in mid-breath when he thought he heard someone whisper his name. His eyes popped open and his body stiffened. Was someone there? He listened intently but heard no further sound. Out of the stillness of the air, an unexpected breeze blew on his face and his tear-soaked cheeks cooled. He wiped them with the backs of his hands, creating streaks of mud across his face. He then crawled to his knees and peeked over the bushes at his back. He didn't see anyone. He was convinced he was now hearing things and losing what was left of his mind.

He slowly rose to his feet and looked at the house. The glass door was closed. He could have sworn he'd left it open. He looked the yard around for Boomer but didn't see him. He whistled. The dog didn't come. He scanned the yard but didn't see anyone.

He looked toward the tree swing and witnessed a bluebird land on a branch on one of the apple trees. He fell back down on the grass and watched as it began to sing. Maybe it was singing for him. Maybe it was a message from Savannah.

Chapter 21

Over the last few weeks, Emma had stopped speaking to all her friends. The phone rang occasionally but she refused to answer it. She knew it would be Sally or one of the girls from school, and she didn't have anything to say to any of them. She spent most of her time in her room with the door closed or sitting on the tree swing with Boomer always nearby.

Just before eight a.m., the school bus arrived right on schedule. Emma had packed her lunch the night before and had been waiting on the front porch for twenty minutes. In previous years, she had never taken the bus, but she was determined to ride it this year. She carefully climbed up the bus steps and took her seat. She kept her head down; she never looked back at the house.

***

August stood in the front doorway, watching her leave, waving and smiling in case she turned around. He wanted to encourage her, to show her that life goes on and one could be happy again, but when she climbed on the bus and didn't look back, he wondered if that were true. He was glad she was becoming more independent. He was pleased she was riding the bus. Maybe that meant she was growing up and would eventually be fine. He certainly hoped so.

***

Savannah stood in the upstairs window, watching the bus rumbled away from the house. She watched it roll down the tree-lined drive and turn on to Beach Road. She watched it until it was out of sight, and she thought about how Emma had lost so much. The poor child seemed to be tipping back and forth between anger and sadness, and Savannah was certain she couldn't do anything to help the girl.

Boomer nudged Savannah's hand with his head, and she reached down and rubbed him behind his ears. He looked up at her and pressed his head closer to her.

"I don't think Emma is the only one who's sad," she whispered. "You seem to need a lot more attention these days, too."

Boomer whined and plopped down on his stomach, looking up at Savannah.

"Even the dog is sad," she thought.

Chapter 22

Friday evening, Emma was practicing the piano in the music room. August loved to hear the house fill with the beautiful sound. His daughter had a great love for music and showed a pronounced aptitude for it. She had been studying weekly with a woman down the street, taking lessons for about three years, and was becoming quite a talented pianist. Tonight, she had been practicing for about thirty minutes, working tirelessly on a new piece of music, but it seemed she had given up on it and was now playing her favorite piece, "Moonlight Sonata" by Beethoven.

August entered the family room and sat down on the flowered sofa by the fireplace. He was engrossed in the melancholy melody as he stared into the dancing fire. The song seemed to match his mood perfectly. The dark piece with its dissonant tones brought tears to his eyes.

He said softly, "I wish you were here, Savannah. I wish all of this were a bad dream."

Tears fell from his eyes as the darkness of the music overtook him.

***

Savannah was seated in the Queen Anne chair in the parlor outside the music room, listening to Emma play. As Emma hit the last chord, Savannah closed her eyes and whispered, "I miss you so much, August."

***

August rose from the sofa, wiped his eyes, and walked out the back door to get some fresh air.

***

Savannah remained in her chair, her heart feeling as if it would break.

Chapter 23

Early Monday morning, August sat on the overstuffed chair in the living room, reading the last of the weekend newspaper. Savannah was in the kitchen, trimming the dead leaves off the herbs that were growing on the window sill. Boomer sauntered into the kitchen and jumped up on the edge of the sink to see if Savannah had anything good for him. Startled, Savannah bumped the sage container and sent it flying to the tile floor. The clay pot shattered and dirt scattered across the floor.

Savannah opened the pantry and flipped on the light so she could retrieve the broom. "Dumb dog, you startled me." She shook her finger at Boomer, who went to lie down on his braided rug in the corner of the kitchen.

She swept up the mess and carted the dirt and broken flower-pot pieces out to the garage to put them in the trash can.

***

At that exact moment, Emma was heading out the front door to go to school.

August caught a glimpse of her in the front hallway and yelled, "You should check on that noise before you go. It's probably your dog making a mess."

But Emma had already slammed the front door, oblivious to the commotion.

August sighed, gathered up the pages of his newspaper, and dropped them on the floor next to the overstuffed chair. He walked into the hallway and stopped for a moment to look out the window as Emma disappeared down the driveway in the yellow school bus. He shook his head, wondering what in the world he could do to help his depressed teenager.

After the bus turned onto the street, he continued into the kitchen to search for the source of the crash. He looked around the island and at the kitchen counters but found nothing amiss. He bent over and looked under the table, but he didn't find anything that would have made the noise. He opened the pantry and saw nothing out of place. He turned off the light and closed the door, pausing for a moment to wonder when he had left the light on. Boomer glanced up at him from his rug in the corner.

"What was that noise, Boomer?"

Boomer, as usual, responded with a wagging tail.

Chapter 24

On a mid-December morning, Mary barged into the house, toting a large casserole dish. She headed straight for the kitchen to place it in the refrigerator. "Hello? Is anyone home?" She didn't hear a response and walked toward the living room. "Hello?"

August simultaneously entered the living room from the back of the house as Mary entered from the front hallway. Savannah was seated on the sofa, reading a book.

"Oh, there you are." Mary busied herself picking up newspapers that were scattered on the floor by the overstuffed chair. "Do you realize you haven't been out of this house for three months? This is just not healthy, and you have to stop it. You need to move on. You know, it's no disrespect to at least try to go on living. You need to at least try."

She got no response but didn't seem to

notice. She finished gathering the newspapers from the floor, folded them, and placed them in a pile on the mahogany desk in the corner. The telephone on the desk blared as she neared it.

"I made you and Emma a chicken casserole, so you can both eat a good dinner tonight," Mary said. The phone rang a second time and she answered, "Ryan residence."

"Mary, the girls called from the bakery and said one of the ovens won't turn on. They need you or me to come fix it right away, and I'm in the middle of something."

"All right, Billy. Call them back and tell them I'll be there in…" She looked at the clock on the desk. "In fifteen minutes."

She hung up and continued her prior conversation without missing a beat. "You two enjoy the casserole tonight, and I'll come back in a few days to help you get this house decorated for the holidays, if not for you, at least for Emma. She can't have a Christmas with no tree and no decorations. I have to run now. Billy said the girls need me at the bakery." Mary moved toward the front door. "I'll come by later, okay?"

Without waiting for an answer, she scampered out the door, and she was gone.

Chapter 25

It seldom snowed in Biloxi, but the clouds looked ominous and full of moisture of the freezing drizzle variety. The dark winter days had killed what was left of the garden. The perennials had turned to dry, brown stalks of misery, and the vegetable plants had yielded the last harvest of their short lifetimes.

August sat in the den at his desk and stared at a picture of the three of them—him, Savannah, and Emma. They were so happy in the photograph, with the whole world ahead of them, a bright future right in the palm of their hands. The picture had been taken last spring, when the plants and trees were just blooming with summer's promise. The three of them were standing in front of the apple tree in the back yard. He remembered that day vividly. Mary had come over to visit and remarked on how lovely the apple tree was. Savannah had agreed, saying it was the most beautiful blooming season she had ever seen, and if every one of those blooms turned into an apple, she would have to make an enormous amount of pies and would be canning apples for weeks. Emma said she had never canned anything before, and Savannah and Mary told her they would teach her come fall. The girls were all smiles and giggles when August told them to stand in front of the tree so he could take their picture. He couldn't remember how it happened, but somehow Mary got the camera and took this picture of the tree of them. It was a glorious day.

As August admired the photo, he noticed Boomer in it. Strangely, he'd never noticed the dog in the picture before. Boomer was sitting next to them and looked like he was smiling, too. August smiled at the dog.

They had picked him out for Emma as a Christmas gift last year. The placed the pup in a box, and Emma laughed hysterically at the box moving and whining. When Emma flipped the top off the box, Boomer jumped out and started licking her face. The two of them rolled around on the floor for hours. August thought Emma would never get the smile off her face. It was the happiest he had ever seen his little girl. They sat around the Christmas tree, playing with the puppy, laughing and drinking eggnog. The fireplace burned brightly, and their home was filled with love and promise. After Emma and Boomer went to bed that night, Savannah and August curled up on the floor in front of the fireplace. They leaned on big pillows against the sofa and admired the Christmas tree.

Savannah whispered to August, "I have a gift for you."

"You and I agreed to not exchange gifts. We have everything we need and more. Why would you get me a gift?" He was a little upset with her for doing what they had agreed not to do. He was also embarrassed that he didn't have a gift for her in return.

She rose, moved to the desk, and pulled something out of the bottom drawer. It was a small box wrapped in plain blue paper, tied with a white ribbon. She held it toward August. "Honey, it's no big deal. I didn't actually buy it for you. It's just a little something I want to give you. Really, it's nothing."

August squinted at her, exhaled in frustration, and reached for the gift. He pulled the white ribbon and peeled back the wrapping. Inside was a wooden box. He opened it, and in the velvet lining he found something blue. He grabbed the string, pulled it out, and saw it was a small glass bird.

"See?" she said. "It's really for both of us."

"It's our little bluebird. It's amazing." He held it by the string and watched it spin in the twinkle of the Christmas tree lights. "Where ever did you find this?"

"I've had it a long time, tucked in the bottom of a chest."

He leaned over, gave her a kiss, and they rose to their feet. They hung the bluebird on a branch and stepped back, with their arms wrapped around each other, to admire it. The fire crackled behind them as "Stardust" began to play softly on the radio. August kissed Savannah on the forehead. "It's perfect and so are you. Thank you," he whispered in her ear.

She laid her head on his shoulder and smiled.

August's attention was brought back to the

photograph as, for the very first time, he noticed that right above Boomer's head, a little bluebird sat on a branch of the apple tree. He pulled the photo close and squinted at it.

"I'll be damned," he said. "Why didn't I ever notice that before?" His eyes filled with tears.

Christmas would have been their four-month anniversary.

✳✳✳

Savannah walked through the hall and stopped to look at the family pictures on the large armoire in the hallway. A melancholy smile formed on her lips. "Oh, I love this picture. I love you, August," she whispered. She picked up the photograph of the two of them, taken the evening they got engaged. He was so handsome, and she was so happy that night. They were supposed to live a long and happy life together. Why didn't that happen? What strange twist of fate pulled them apart yet again? A tear rolled down her face as she traced the cheek of her dear August with her finger. A tapping noise snapped her out of her reverie, and she walked toward the front door to look out the window.

✳✳✳

August also heard the noise. He rose from his desk, walked toward the window, and pulled aside the heavy curtains to look outside. Light snowflakes had begun to fall, making the front yard look like a fairy tale. The green grass was now white, and the branches of the bare trees looked like a postcard. On the lowest branch of the tree nearest the front door sat a bluebird. Though it was quite late in the season to witness a bluebird in the yard, there it was. August stared at it in awe.

The bird looked back and forth from the window of the den to the window of the front door.

Yes, indeed, a bluebird in the front yard in the middle of a rare snowfall.

Chapter 26

As promised, Mary came back to the house to decorate it for the holidays. Billy had set up a Christmas tree and Mary got busy decorating that as well. When Emma saw the holiday display, she didn't look much impressed. Mary had hoped Emma's sadness would turn around a little as the holiday season neared, but that didn't seem to be happening. She thought it best to get Emma involved in the decorating, so she asked Emma to help her trim the tree. As they placed ornaments on the branches, Mary offered to take Emma out for a late dinner.

"I appreciate the offer, but I promised Sally I would spend the night. I haven't really spent any time with her the last couple months, and it's the first day of our holiday break from school."

Mary's shoulders drooped.

Emma noticed her aunt's change in demeanor and added, "Maybe we can go to lunch tomorrow."

Mary nodded and smiled. "That would be wonderful. I'd love to spend some time with you. We can go into town early and have lunch and…"

Emma reached for the next ornament from the box—a little glass bird. She held it in front of her face.

"What's that?" Mary asked.

"I don't know. I've never seen it before."

"Oh, how sweet. That reminds me of a story my father told us when we were little. He was in New Orleans while he was courting our mother and a gypsy woman told him a story about the bluebird being the symbol for true love. She said if you see a bluebird when you're with the one you love, you will be with that person forever. The next day, he was with our mother and they saw a bluebird. The rest is history." Mary reached for the ornament and Emma handed it to her. She looked down at it and said, "I wonder if Savannah bought this ornament because of that story."

***

After a few hours of decorating, Emma and Mary finished and both left for the night, leaving the house eerily silent. The only sounds were the crackle of the fireplace and the soft music coming from the small radio on the mantel.

August sat on the sofa and stared at the Christmas tree. *It's beautiful*, he thought. The girls did a great job trimming the tree and decorating, and the house did look a lot happier. He hoped it would brighten Emma's spirits. He didn't know if anything would brighten his.

As "The Way You Look Tonight" came on the radio, he noticed the glass bluebird ornament right in the middle of the tree. It brought a smile to his face. "Where in the world did you find that?" he asked, wishing he'd pushed Savannah more about where the bauble came from.

✳✳✳

Savannah sat on the overstuffed chair on the opposite side of the fireplace, and she too noticed the little bluebird. She thought about her strange encounter with the old woman on the beach in New Orleans. She knew the bluebird was an unusual gift, but the old woman had known far too much about her to not be taken seriously. The crone had told her, "It is my gift to you to guard against the pain of the future. You only need to ask, and your wish will be granted." Even though the thought of the old woman sent chills up Savannah's spine, she smiled as she stared at the glass bird.

"I should have told you that story, August," she said out loud. "There are so many things I want to tell you, so much I need to say."

Near the top of the tree, on one of the highest branches, hung three little glass bells, nestled inside each other, that tinkled at the slightest of movements. Savannah had bought them last year to use as a warning if the puppy started causing mischief with the Christmas tree. The bells tinkled many times last year.

But at this moment, the bells began to tinkle and Boomer was nowhere to be seen.

***

August looked up at the bells. They tinkled a second time.

"Why would those make noise right now? There must be an open window somewhere," he thought. But he knew that couldn't be true. It had been so cold; he hadn't opened a window in the house for at least a couple of weeks.

The bells tinkled a third time.

August stood and walked over to the tree and reached up toward the bells. He held his hand there for a moment, checking for a breeze. No, no breeze. He bent over and looked under the tree. It looked stable, not crooked or leaning. Then his eye caught the glass bluebird again.

He started to cry. "Savannah, I miss you so much."

***

Savannah also walked over to the tree and looked up at the bells. Then she too found herself staring at the bluebird, which was eye level for her.

"Oh, August, why does it have to be this way?" she whispered.

"I don't know how much more of this I can take," said August.

"I can't bear another moment of it," Savannah said.

They stood in front of the beautiful tree and shed tears—tears of grief, tears of pain, of sadness, and loneliness.

"How am I supposed to get through the

holidays without you?" Savannah murmured.

"How am I supposed to move on?" August said.

The fireplace popped loudly behind Savannah and she jumped. She turned to look at the fire. August did, too.

The bells tinkled again and they both turned back to the tree. Savannah touched the bluebird and said, "I don't know if the gypsy woman was right, but I wish I could talk to you one more time. I wish this bluebird could make that happen."

The radio station changed songs and the beginning strains of "Stardust" filled the room. It became warm and humid as a blue mist crept out slowly from under the tree. It spread across the floor and grew and swirled around the tree in a circular shape, like storm clouds in a slow-moving hurricane. The swirling increased as Savannah and August watched, mystified. It engulfed the entire tree and everything outside the mist grew fuzzy, as if it had been absorbed into a glass of dark liquid. The sofa and the fireplace became wavy, like great heat on desert sand. Savannah and August were enveloped in the mist. They both looked around in amazement at the mist. The tree remained clear, but the rest of the room seemed distant, and "Stardust" sounded like it was echoing from a far-away tunnel.

August's and Savannah's eyes met.

"Savannah?" August murmured.

Savannah stared at him. "How is this possible?"

He held out his hand and she gently touched his fingers. They stared at each other for a long time. Finally, he pulled her into his arms and they held each other tightly.

She broke their embrace and backed up a step. She looked at the bluebird. "This is what I wished for."

"It was my wish, too." He reached for her and kissed her hands one at a time.

"You don't understand. The gypsy woman who gave me that bluebird said it held a wish, and I wished to talk to you one more time." She threw her arms around his neck and he hugged her hard. "I miss you so much, August. I've been drowning in memories and what-ifs and why-nots and could-have-beens."

They held each other without speaking for a long, long time. The blue mist swirled around them in a hazy vortex. Finally her knees couldn't hold her weight any longer and she lowered herself down onto the rug in front of the tree. August didn't let her go as he fell to his knees next to her.

"I don't understand how this is happening," he said.

"It's the wish. It's the gypsy woman. She said I would need it someday. I guess this is what she was talking about."

August's eyes misted. "Savannah, I'm so sorry about what happened at our wedding. It was all my fault."

"August, what are you talking about? There was no wedding."

August wrinkled his brow. "Of course there was. We danced."

She shook her head. "No, we didn't dance. You never made it."

"I don't understand. I remember seeing you in

your dress."

"August, when I got to the church, the police came and told me you had been shot at your office."

He shook his head. "Yes, I remember a shooting at the office, but I didn't die, a gypsy man died." He paused for a moment, trying to piece together the events of that fateful day. "I tried to get out of the building, but a policeman told me to go back into my office. He said there was a gunman...yes, Bernard Corning, one of the gypsies was in the building with a gun."

"August, Bernard Corning shot you."

"No, that's impossible. I saw him get shot by the policeman. I heard the policeman on the phone calling for help. I heard a woman scream...I was...I was lying on the floor. It was Nancy...Nancy's voice I heard scream. She yelled for someone to call a doctor." Abruptly, he looked down at his chest and rubbed his shirt. He looked back up at Savannah in disbelief. "I had blood on my hands. I was shot?"

"Yes, you were shot. You never made it to the church." Savannah began crying.

"I remember Nancy whispering to me to hang on. She said I couldn't die, that I had to hang on, that I had to get to the church, that you were waiting for me in your beautiful wedding dress. She described the way it sparkled. She said we would dance all night under the stars."

"It didn't happen, August."

He shook his head. "It didn't happen? I must have gotten her words and reality mixed up in my head. I could have sworn we danced."

She sadly looked down and shook her head. "We didn't dance."

They sat quietly for a while, while each tried to come to terms with their own realities.

Savannah broke the silence. "When I was a teenager, I spoke to a gypsy woman in New Orleans, who said her son, Bernard, would have a run-in with you. How did she know that?"

August shrugged. "Was it the same woman who gave you the bluebird?"

Savannah looked at him strangely, as if all the pieces had suddenly fallen together. "Yes, it was the same woman who told my dad the bluebird story, the same woman who gave me that bluebird and told me it held a wish." She pointed up to the Christmas tree. "I think she loved my dad. I wonder if Bernard was my dad's child."

"I remember looking at him on the floor. He looked a lot like you. He had the same hair."

Savannah's eyes were as big as saucers. "I don't think the bluebird is magical. I think it's a curse. It separated the gypsy woman and my dad, and in some twisted fate, her son...their son has now separated us."

They stared into each other's eyes and held hands until the sun began to rise. When the first light of day began to stream through the window, Savannah pulled her hands away. "August, this has been so hard. I can't sit here and pretend that everything is all right, when we know it's not." She sat up a little straighter. For the first time in her life, she felt like the decision was in her hands. For the first time ever, she did not feel the urge to run. She was not a product of fate. Her life would be her choice, not some gypsy curse. She hadn't been old enough to decide where she would live when her father died.

She hadn't even been in control of her own wedding day. But today, a decision needed to be made, and it would be her decision and hers alone.

August recognized the determination that crossed her face and let out a sigh. "Savannah," he said softly, "please know that I love you more than anything in this world. I love you more than life itself. You are my soul, my heart, my whole existence. I don't want to hold you back. I don't want you to be a prisoner to the past. I want nothing more than for you to be happy. That's all that matters to me."

Savannah kept her eyes on August. She felt something shift inside her when the reality of the words reached her ears. Yes, it was time to stop dwelling on the past and start looking toward the future. She suddenly knew something bigger was in store for her. Something important lay in her future, something she had to do alone. Why else would they have been separated…again? Why else would all this have happened?

"August, it breaks my heart to say I think our time together was not for us," she said through her tears. "I think I'm supposed to be here for Emma." She sat still as a statue as he faced her. He calmly looked into her eyes and her tears stopped flowing and a sense of peace settled into her heart.

He nodded. "I don't know what Emma's future holds, but I'm sure, somehow, you're a part of it."

"I don't want Emma to face being uprooted and living with different family. My part in this relationship is to raise your daughter."

August glanced up at the bluebird.

"I think you're right. Please take care of her. I

want you both to be happy." He cupped her chin and looked into her eyes. "Please know that I will love you forever and ever. I have loved you since we were children, and I will love you for all of eternity."

Boomer barked at the back door to be let outside. August and Savannah rose and, hand in hand, they walked to the glass door. They both reached for the door handle at the same time. They opened the door together and looked at each other as Boomer ran past them, frolicking in the snowflakes, barking and wagging his tail.

August looked at the gentle snowflakes covering the yard.

Savannah held her hand over her mouth and willed herself not to cry.

"I guess it's time, Savannah," August whispered as he squeezed her hand. "I will always love you."

Savannah blinked her eyes as the tears came. August slowly released her hand, and she watched him walked onto the patio, down the steps, onto the snow-covered lawn, and out across the yard, into the light.

Savannah wiped the tears from her face as Boomer ran to her side and sat next to her. She absentmindedly patted his head, and he whined.

"It's okay, boy, it's going to be okay," she told him as she stared at the horizon.

He barked and ran toward the pantry.

She closed the door and followed him to the pantry to get him a treat. She sat down on the floor with him as he gobbled up his treat and gave her a sloppy kiss on the cheek. She felt a sense of peace she hadn't felt in a long time. She took in a deep breath and released it.

"Merry Christmas, Boomer."

He barked.

Chapter 13
August 25, 1936,
1:00 p.m.

August placed a gentle hand on Nancy's shoulder and told her to stay put in his office until the police said it was safe to come out. He grabbed his suit coat, inched open his office door, and stepped into the outer office. At that very moment, the ding of the elevator sounded and a police officer emerged and spotted him between the partitions.

"Please go back into your office and close the door, sir. The suspect is loose in the building."

August backed up a foot toward his office. "Loose in the building?"

"Yes, sir."

Just then, the stairwell door flew open. A crazed man bolted out of the stairwell and stopped when he saw August. The man looked around wildly, but with the partition at his back, he didn't see the policeman standing on the other side. The man was dressed in dirty trousers and a wrinkled shirt with stains on the front. His beard hung long, as well as his hair. August instantly knew the man was the gypsy the police were looking for.

The officer stood on the other side of the partition, out of the man's line of sight, but the officer saw the surprised look on August's face. He pulled his gun and swiftly rounded the corner.

"*Freeze!*" the officer yelled.

The man pulled his gun from behind his back and waved it wildly in the air.

A woman screamed at the far end of the hall and the man looked in that direction. He ran toward the voice, passing Nancy's desk and running right between the police officer and August.

"*FREEZE!*" the officer yelled again.

Shots were fired, followed by more screams.

And it was over as fast as it had begun.

The gunman lay on the floor, unmoving, in front of Nancy's desk, blood staining his shirt from the wound in his chest. It had also splattered on the rug, turning it from soft beige to a spotted burgundy. The officer cautiously approached with his gun still aimed at the man. He kicked the man's gun from his hand, patted him down for any other weapons, pulled his wallet from his pocket, and flipped it open. Then he grabbed the telephone from Nancy's desk.

"The suspect is down on the sixth floor. Repeat, the suspect has been shot and is down on the sixth floor." He read from the man's wallet. "His name is Bernard Corning."

August couldn't decipher the rest of what the

officer was saying. He drifted in and out of consciousness as he lay on the floor about twenty feet from Bernard Corning. Nancy emerged from his office and screamed when she saw him on the floor. She fell to her knees and cradled August's head in her hands. "Mr. Ryan, Mr. Ryan, hang on, you'll be all right."

August looked up at her for a moment and then closed his eyes.

"Mr. Ryan, listen to me! Focus on my voice. Your lovely bride is waiting for you. You have to hang on. She's dressed in her white wedding gown and waiting for you at the church. Tonight, you'll dance to the orchestra, and your bride will sparkle like a rare diamond. You need to hang on, Mr. Ryan. "

August felt a pain in his chest and sluggishly reached up to touch it with his hand. He held his hand in front of his face to see why it was wet. It was red—covered in blood. His blood. His vision began to dim and he heard Nancy yell, "Someone call a doctor!"

Chapter 27

Savannah and Emma sat on the swing in the garden, enjoying the warmth of the spring afternoon. Emma threw a stick and Boomer ran like lightning to retrieve it. The daffodils and lilies had bloomed. Peach, pink, and yellow surrounded them, and the air was filled with the sweetest fragrance.

"So, how's school?" Savannah asked.

"Okay, I guess," replied Emma. "It's hard to get through some days. Some of the other kids don't talk to me anymore. I know they're not trying to be rude; they just don't know what to say. And sometimes the teachers look at me like I'm a lost little puppy. I don't want them to feel sorry for me. It's just hard, you know?"

"Yeah, I know. That will all fade in time, I hope."

Savannah had been Emma's age when she lost her father. She knew there was nothing she could say that would make it any easier for the girl. She was, however, determined to keep Emma's life as normal as possible and not do anything drastic like pull the child out of school and move her to New Orleans. August's estate had left enough money to maintain Emma's lifestyle until she graduated from college. Savannah was going to stay right here and make that happen.

She was certain that's what the purpose of her life was supposed to be. She was to be Emma's caretaker because she understood the pain of losing a parent. She wasn't supposed to be with August, only to raise his daughter.

"The apple blossoms look so pretty this time of year, and I bet we'll have a ton of apples this year so we can make pies again," Emma said.

Savannah nodded and looked over toward the apple trees. They were full of blooms, looking like they did the time she and August first saw the bluebird.

"I miss my dad," Emma said.

Sitting on the lowest branch of the nearest apple tree was a tiny bluebird.

"So do I, honey, so do I."

Savannah watched the bird and smiled.

The End

About the Author

Lori Crane was born and raised in Meridian, Mississippi and now lives in greater Nashville, Tennessee. She is a member of the Daughters of the American Revolution, the United States Daughters of 1812, and the United Daughters of the Confederacy. She's also a professional musician and member of Screen Actors Guild-American Federation of Radio and Television Artists.

Please visit Lori's website
www.LoriCrane.com

Bibliography

Okatibbee Creek Series

Okatibbee Creek
An Orphan's Heart
Elly Hays

Stuckey's Bridge Trilogy

The Legend of Stuckey's Bridge
Stuckey's Legacy: The Legend Continues
Stuckey's Gold: The Curse of Lake Juzan

The Culpepper Saga

I, John Culpepper
John Culpepper the Merchant
John Culpepper, Esquire
Culpepper's Rebellion

Other Titles by Lori Crane

Savannah's Bluebird
Witch Dance
The Culpepper-Fairfax Scandal
On This Day: A Perpetual Calendar for Family Genealogy